'At a time when hom⁓ ... of Africa, and barely feat⁓ ... ̓is book is a welcome ... ̓tories, Osman writes ⁓ ... ⁓ıties are shaped as much ... ⁓ıtural origins... Osman is a courag⁓ ... ⁓ an original one. His language is pepper⁓ ... ⁓ords and crafted with all the concision and r. ... ⁓oetry. At a time when African writing is on the rise, ⁓ɪan stands above the crowd.'

BERNARDINE EVARISTO, *The Independent*

'One of the great joys of reading is finding books that detail experiences not often seen in mainstream literature. *Fairytales for Lost Children* by Diriye Osman is a raw collection of short stories about the queer Somali experience. These are often stories about exile from family, from country, from sanity, from self. Osman works well within the fairytale tradition. He uses patois and slang and rhythmic cadence to tell these stories in the only language they can be told... the power of these stories is undeniable.'

ROXANE GAY, *The Nation*

'Osman's work exhibits a startlingly original voice that will surely challenge many within the Somali community, not noted for its openness about sexual identity, whilst surprising readers most familiar with the East African country for reports on Islamic militants and piracy.'

MAGNUS TAYLOR, *The New Internationalist*

'A series of poetic vignettes that utilize personal history, national trauma, vernacular, and linguistic sound patterning as texture, this book weaves together personal narratives of queer refugees—from the mother of the lesbian Somali daughter who casts her dreams into the ocean on paper and bits of rock, to the trans woman nurse in the psych ward who manipulates the medical industrial system for her own safety, to the desperate drag queen femme boy who slides on those first silk stockings, this book follows them all... *Fairytales for Lost Children* is a must-read for anyone, displaced or not, who has suffered the blessing and curse of coming out as queer in a world not ready to receive it. Texturally beautiful and tonally gorgeous, Osman has created a dark world of language and culture that every lost child can find themselves in.'

JULY WESTHALE, *Lambda Literary Review*

'Osman's triumphant first book is a testament to just what can happen when a queer person gets up, gets out and gets something. Though his characters face plenty of painful challenges — homophobia, anti-refugee prejudice, mental illness — Osman's stories are suffused with the possibility of joy and pleasure, whether in the form of sexual awakening, gender exploration or in learning how to stand up for yourself. Ultimately, his fairytales are affirmations of why life is worth living, even for the lost. The book's final story, about a gay Somali-Jamaican couple living in London, concludes: 'We own our bodies. We own our lives.''

JAMESON FITZPATRICK, *Next Magazine*

'Set in Somalia, Kenya and London, these stories are concerned with identity, self-realization, displacement and the bonds of family. Osman's vivid and intimate style brings to life narratives rooted in his own experiences as a gay Somali.'

EDEN WOOD, *Diva*

'Narrated by young gay and lesbian Somalis, Diriye Osman's *Fairytales For Lost Children* is a rich, complex and lyrical set of tales that span the complexities of family, identity and the immigrant experience. Set in Kenya, Somalia and South London, this collection of stories is sure to move and enthral in equal measure. One to watch out for.'

WILL DAVIS, *Attitude*

'Each of Osman's characters has been written into emancipation, whether it be erupting, a gentle acceptance, or falling quietly — like snow in fog. This book is also a record of the physical, mental and emotional effects of conservative power, pressure and prejudice on his richly resistant and defiant characters. In totality we are presented with an exhibition of loss: innocence, fear, family, shame, virginity, love and belonging. But what is lost leaves the space for something more precious, sacred and transformative. Something necessary. The freedom to explore your own ways of being with ownership — that as the last line of the collection states — 'We own our bodies. We own our lives.'

JONATHAN DUNCAN, *Africa Is A Country*

'An abundance of styles and sensory impressions...these bittersweet stories are painfully beautiful. Yet in amongst all the sadness of exile and repudiation there is always an emphasis on lust, joy and pleasure. Osman's writing seems to be a carousel of languages, scents, melodies and flavours which celebrates beauty.'

ANNA JÄGER, *Chimurenga*

FAIRYTALES
FOR
LOST CHILDREN

DIRIYE OSMAN

Published September 2013 by Team Angelica Publishing, an
imprint of Angelica Entertainments Ltd

TEAM
ANGELICA

www.teamangelica.com

A CIP catalogue record for this book is available from the
British Library

ISBN 978-0-9569719-4-4

Printed and bound by Lightning Source

Grateful acknowledgement is made to the following publica-
tions where these stories first appeared in slightly different
forms: *Poetry Review*, 'Watering The Imagination'; *The Queer
African Reader* and *Under The Influence*, 'Tell The Sun Not To
Shine'; *Jungle Jim*, 'Fairytales For Lost Children'; *Attitude*,
'Shoga'; *SCARF* and *Attitude*, 'If I Were A Dance'; *Prospect*,
'Pavilion'; *Bedford Square 5*, 'Ndambi'; *Kwani?*, 'Earthling' and
'Your Silence Will Not Protect You'.

For John R. Gordon

When I dare to be powerful – to use my strength in the service of my vision – it becomes less and less important whether I am afraid.

– AUDRE LORDE

TABLE OF CONTENTS

سقيم الخيال

WATERING THE IMAGINATION

 have spent my whole life living near the coast of Bosaaso, Somalia. I don't know any other land. While the boat people, those who are hungry for new homes in places like London and Luxembourg, risk their lives on cargo ships, I stand firm on this soil and I tell stories. I tell stories to my daughters about kings and warrior queens, freedom-fighters and poets. I tell these stories to remind my children and myself that Somalia is fertile with history and myth. The only seed that needs regular watering is our imagination.

My eldest daughter, Suldana, is in love with another woman. She is eighteen and she spends her days working at our kiosk selling milk and eggs, and at night she sneaks out and goes down to the beach to see her lover. She crawls back into bed at dawn, smelling of sea and salt and perfume.

Suldana is beautiful and she wraps this beauty around herself like a shawl of stars. When she smiles her dimples deepen and you can't help but be charmed. When she walks down the street men stare and whistle and ache. But they cannot have her. Every day marriage proposals arrive with offers of high dowries but I wave them away. We never talk about these things like mothers and daughters should; but I respect her privacy and I allow her to live.

In Somali culture many things go unsaid: how we love, who we love and why we love that way. I don't know why Suldana loves the way she does. I don't know why she loves who she does. But I do know that by respecting her privacy I am letting her dream in a way that my generation was not capable of. I'm letting her reach for something neither one of us can articulate.

So we take our voices and our stories to the sea. Every evening we walk towards the water and we write our hopes and dreams on scraps of paper. We wrap the paper around stones and tie it on with rubber bands. We then fling those stones that carry our hopes and dreams into the ocean. My mother and my mother's mother used to do this. To us it's a way of expressing some of the things we cannot verbalise. It's a way of sharing our most intimate secrets without shame or fear. In doing so, we have created our own mythology and history.

Suldana must take that history and forge her own future. And when she does go forth, I will honour my promise as her parent and go forth with her. We will not turn back.

TELL THE SUN NOT TO SHINE

It was Eid and I had no one to celebrate it with. I needed a sign to point me either east or west. The sign came as a leaflet through my letterbox. It was an invitation to Eid prayer at Peckham Mosque. The sign pointed south so I headed there.

At the mosque everyone was in their Eid best. The Asian and Somali men wore their best khamiises in grey and white. The Nigerian men were dressed like sapeurs – shirts the colour of flamingos, shoes made from crocodile-skin. The Asian and Somali women wore their best garbas and jilbabs in grey and black. The Nigerian women were dressed like beauty queens – dresses the colour of Fanta, shoes with clear heels. The children all ran around with Nike ticks and leaping Pumas on their backs.

I went to the taps outside to perform ablution. An Asian kid in a dove-gray khamiis guided me.

'Go like this,' he said, washing his hands and wrists three times. I noticed he had bite marks on his toffee-brown wrists. I copied him.

'Go like this,' he said, rinsing his mouth three times. I noticed his bottom lip was purple and fat like a plum. I copied him.

'Go like this,' he said, drawing water into his nose and then blowing it out three times. I noticed his nose had a cut the colour of pastrami across its bridge. I copied him.

After ablution, it was time to pray. 'Go,' the boy said. So I went.

I placed my shoes by the door. The mosque smelt of

feet, cologne and samosas. The carpet felt like moss and the walls were white. A chipped chandelier hung from the ceiling. The men sat near the imam's podium; there was a partition for the women at the back. I crouched next to a man with Jheri curls. He had six toes on his left foot. When he wriggled his toes, the sixth one didn't move.

'Eid Mubarak, my brother,' he said.

'Eid Mubarak,' I said.

'I hope you find peace,' he said, sensing my sadness.

'I hope so too,' I said. I wondered if his sixth toe gave him a sixth sense.

The imam called out 'Allahu Akbar! Allahu Akbar!' Everyone stood up and raised their hands to their ears. Even though the imam's back was turned to me, I recognised his voice instantly. It was Libaan. He was wearing an egg-white khamiis and skullcap. His baritone was still as smooth as water.

As he said 'Allahu Akbar' once more I remembered the first time we'd met. He had come from Somalia to spend the summer with us in Nairobi. I was fourteen, he was eighteen.

The loudspeaker crackled as he now recited Surah Al-Fatiha. His voice swooped and dived like a kite around the Arabic syllables.

I remembered him towering over me. His skin was dark like Oreos. He had two gold teeth. He introduced me to cigarettes. I would choke on the smoke and he would say, 'You'll get there, kid.' Now I smoke twenty a day.

After Al-Fatiha, he recited Surah Lahab.

I remembered giving him my bed and sleeping on the floor. We would stay up late and he would tell me about being a goatherd in Somalia. I told him about my school in Nairobi and how everyone there called me a refugee. 'Next time,' he said, 'I'll come to your school and beat them up.'

When he said 'Allahu Akbar!' we all bowed.

I remembered the first time I saw him naked. He was sleeping and his bed-sheet had slipped down, revealing his buttocks. My heart pounded. I leant closer. I wanted to touch him but was terrified. I sat next to him on the bed and he didn't wake up. I touched his buttocks with trembling fingers and ran out of the room. When I came back he was still sleeping. I squeezed his buttocks gently and ran out of the room. When I came back he was still sleeping. I tried to finger him but without opening his eyes he growled, 'For fuck's sake! I'm trying to get some sleep!' I ran out of the room.

My face heated up now as he stood and said, 'Allah hears those who praise Him.' I said, 'Praise be to you, our Lord,' in a low tone.

I was afraid he'd tell my parents. But instead the next day he had offered me a Malboro. We snuck out of the back of the house and smoked in silence. When we were done he ruffled my hair and smiled a gold-toothed smile that said, 'Let's not mention this.' I couldn't look him in the eye.

Now he boomed 'Allahu Akbar' and the whole congregation prostrated. He said 'Allahu Akbar' again and we prostrated once more.

Instead of going to bed that night Libaan had lowered himself onto my mattress and slid his hand under my blanket. His hand gripped my penis. I was hard. His movements were slow, deliberate. His palms felt as smooth as buttermilk. He smelt of cigarettes and cherry bubblegum. He stroked me until my thighs were moist, my throat dry. When I came, he wiped his hands on my trousers and crawled back into his bed. I went to sleep satisfied and scared and hopeful.

Libaan called out 'Allahu Akbar' and began reciting Surah Al-Fatiha.

The next day we'd played football with the neighbourhood kids. Libaan kept passing me the ball. Every time he did this, he smiled a gold-toothed smile that said, 'Nothing happened.' He was trying to dodge a life of complications. But at night he would place his hands, lips, tongue inside my world of complications. We would catch strokes until it was time for morning prayers. And then we would go about our day wondering if the previous night even happened.

As the prayer came to an end Libaan drew his face to the right and said, 'Asalamu aleykum wa Rahmatullah,' and then to the left and did the same. We followed suit.

On the night before he returned to Somalia we lay together on my dirty mattress. I pressed his palm on my lips. He kissed my collarbone. In the moonlit room I could see him smiling a gold-toothed smile that said, 'Nothing even matters.' As the time for morning prayer came he whispered in my ear, 'Tell the sun not to shine.' I whispered, 'I will if you promise to stay.' He boarded a plane to Somalia the next day.

Now he turned around and began to give a lecture but I wasn't listening. All I noticed was his belly, which was round like a basketball. All I noticed were his cheeks, which drooped like a bulldog's jowls. He still had two gold teeth but the rest were black. His beard had been hennaed until it resembled a bush on fire.

'May Allah bless you and your family on this joyous day,' he was saying. 'May you find peace and comfort and a sense of fulfilment. Amin.'

'Amin,' the congregation said before getting up and heading for the door. As people filtered out I felt an urge to speak to Libaan.

I wanted to tell him that I once dated an Irishman named Simon.

I wanted to tell him that I saw his face whenever I made love to Simon.

I wanted to tell him that my parents disowned me when I came out to them.

I wanted to vomit these words out.

But before I could, a woman in an ink-black jilbab and a young boy dressed in a khamiis walked up to Libaan. He hugged the woman and lifted the boy onto his shoulders. That's when he saw me. He tried to smile a gold-toothed smile that said many things: 'Not here, not now'; 'I'm sorry'; 'I'm scared'. But before he could do it, before he could break my heart a million times over, I did what I knew best.

I ran.

حكايات لأطفال ضائعين

FAIRYTALES FOR LOST CHILDREN

We lived in a sky-blue bungalow on Tigoni Road, right next to Aziza's kindergarten, Little Woods. Although our house was on a decent plot of land the garden was neglected, and thorns and brambles had taken root. I knew fruit and flowers weren't on Hooyo and Aabo's minds. They were thinking bills and blood-relatives that needed beso.

I remembered our garden in Somalia, with its guava and pawpaw trees, callas and azaleas. I often used to sit there and watch bullfrogs hunt insects. In Disney fairytales the bad guy always loses, but in reality he is rarely thwarted. Whenever the bullfrog's tongue flicked out, it rolled back with its victim. I learnt not to mess with nature from an early age.

I was ten years old when I started kindergarten. Aabo and Hooyo thought it was the best way to learn the language.

'But I don't want to learn Ingriis,' I moaned, dunking my margarine sandwich into a cup of tea and slurping it. Aabo finished his porridge and washed it down with a glass of lemon water.

'You have to learn the luuqad,' he said. 'We're in Kenya now. Everyone here speaks English, even the maid.'

'Besides, Aziza is enjoying her school,' said Hooyo, who was polishing my Bata Prefect shoes, adding, 'She's already learning her ABCs.'

This irked me: Aziza surpassing me in the alphabet

was a sign that she would surpass me in life. I grabbed my Aladdin lunchbox, which my mother had stuffed with rice and lamb from the previous night, and followed my dad outside to his Toyota Cressida. It was a poor cousin to the Mercedes we'd owned in Somalia but we were lucky to have a car at all. Seven months ago we were living in Utanga Refugee Camp in Mombasa, unsure of whether we would be sent back to Somalia. I could never forget the corpse of a woman we saw as we drove out of Mogadishu, brains splattered across the roadside. I vomited in the back of the pickup truck because Aabo refused to pull over and let me out.

'I will not stop until we get to the boats,' he shouted, honking at the refugees trying to walk their way out of war. Young men pushed their grandparents in wheelbarrows; a woman in labour was squatting in the middle of the road to give birth.

I thought of that woman now as I glanced at Hooyo's watermelon-sized belly, as she waved goodbye to Aabo and me.

As soon as we got into the car Aabo put on his favourite UB40 cassette, belting out the lyrics to *Red, Red Wine* as we drove down Chaka Road.

'Join me,' he encouraged.

'Okay.'

I sang along in a tinny voice.

'That's terrible. You've got to sing like you mean it.'

'But I do.'

'Then show it.' He lifted his voice to an operatic note. When I tried to copy him, I sounded like Shirley Temple with constipation.

'You'll get there, son,' said Aabo, knowing that I wouldn't. It was nice that he half-believed in me.

We turned down Marcus Garvey Road. At the top of the road was an office building called Studio House, all slick with sunlight bouncing off its black glass panels. Right next to the building were a group of chokoras around my age. They were rummaging through the mountain of rubbish piled outside it, finding the odd banana or orange peel to gnaw on. Their fakhrinimo reminded me of the folks we had seen in the refugee camp, except these boys had bottles of glue clamped between their teeth. Snot slid down from one of the boys' noses. He licked it off.

Because Marcus Garvey was a dirt road Aabo had to go slow and manoeuvre the car carefully to avoid a flat tyre. One of the chokoras saw me staring at him and pointed his middle finger at me. I turned away, afraid. Seven months ago, running around the camp in rags handed to me by UNICEF aid workers, I didn't look much different from those street boys. I was afraid that our newfound prosperity was a trick played by a capricious God: that soon we would be back in Utanga, leading qashin lives that no amount of praying or chanting surahs could elevate.

Aabo had no such worries. He was a man rarely plagued by self-doubt. This was to be expected from a former politician. During Siad Barre's regime Aabo served as one of his chief advisors. Before that he had been the dean of faculty at Somalia National University. And before his prodigious academic and political career he was a shepherd tending his father's flock in Bosaaso. His favourite motto was, 'Life's all about public relations.' It was this cocksure attitude that got us out of Utanga and into a three-bedroom house in Kilimani within months of our arrival there. It was also the same attitude which, coupled with several handy contacts, enabled him to start Pharmcon, his own pharmaceutical company.

He was still singing as the car continued to bump into potholes. Every time the Cressida jolted his voice quavered, but remained rhythmic. Aabo saw life as one long tune. Even during prayer, when he said 'Allahu Akbar' his voice would drip with melisma. As we neared the school I began to worry he would burst into song when he introduced me to my teacher. Luckily he stopped singing when we turned into Kindaruma road and a large pinecone hit the windshield.

'Shit.' Aabo stopped the car. We both got out and looked above. Pine trees towered over us. Thud! Another pinecone hit the roof of the Cressida. Dark figures moved in the trees. Before we knew it, baboons were pelting us with pinecones, primatial terrorists, intimidating us with scary teeth and screeches. Aabo and I hurriedly got back into the car and drove off. We had gone all of thirty feet when he stopped at a compound with a pine tree sign outside it. My heart sank when he said, 'Welcome to Pine Tree Kindergarten.'

'Everyone, please welcome Hirsi,' said my new teacher, Miss Mumbi. 'He's from Somalia.' All I understood were my name and 'Somalia.' Everything else was an alien speech-bubble. Even the way she said my name was exotic: 'Hirsi' not 'Xirsi.' Still, the class, a set of well-fed six-year olds, welcomed me with cheers. They were practically cherubs, ripe for beating. A Kenyan girl with a kuus-kuus hairstyle looked at me like I was a cannibal ready to suck her dhuux dry. If there was a God He would've snatched me from that kindergarten and whisked me back home to people I knew and understood. I began to lose my faith that day.

Miss Mumbi, however, kept hers: not in Pine Tree's educational curriculum, or even in God, but in the teachings of the Mau Mau. She was a militant nationalist posing as a pre-school teacher. Clad in a kanga, she saw the alphabet as the perfect way to decolonise our Disney-addled minds. Whilst other pre-schoolers were learning that 'A' was for 'Apple,' 'B' for 'Ball,' 'C' for 'Cat,' we were grappling with 'A' is for 'Ameru,' 'B' for 'Bukusi,' 'C' for 'Chonyi.' Miss Mumbi listed Kenyan languages and clans that confused us: 'Kore', 'Maragoli,' 'Pokomo.' I hardly knew English, let alone what Pokomo meant. The only English word she used was 'Queen.' She turned to the girls and said, 'You're all queens, my dears.' To which an Indian boy piped to general laughter, 'Can I be a queen, too?'

Even Story Time was political. Miss Mumbi infused each fairytale with Kenyan flavour. She illustrated these remixes on the blackboard. 'Rapunzel' became 'Rehema,' a fly gabar imprisoned in Fort Jesus. Rehema had an Afro that grew and grew. Her Afro grew bigger than her body and she looked bomb. The Afro became so strong that it burst through the ceiling of the fort. It exploded into the sky and reached the stars. The Afro wrapped itself around the moon and pulled Rehema out of the fort.

'When Rehema grew up,' said Miss Mumbi, 'she told the story to her children, and they passed it on to theirs. Even after her death, the Afro lived on.'

To demonstrate this durability, Miss Mumbi patted her own perfect 'fro.

'I want an Afro,' said a white girl with pigtails.

'Then tell your mum. In fact, tell all your mums you want Afros.'

I suspected Miss Mumbi was getting tipsy on power.

'Tomorrow,' she said, 'I shall read you Jomo and the Beanstalk.'

Afterwards the class went outside to play. In the trees baboons screeched 'OoOoAhAh.' I couldn't see them but they sounded close. I imagined a baboon swinging from the branches and landing in the playground. The kids would scream and bolt but the baboon would be too quick. It would snatch a boy and drag him back to the trees. The baboon would season the boy like nyama choma, add salt and paprika, and gobble him up. Then it would toss the bones into the playground as a warning.

I didn't want to be baboon-bait so I headed into the library, where shelves were stacked with Disney buugaag that made me ache. I ran my hand across the spine of each title, savouring its elegance. To me they were holy texts, each idea and image sacred. These stories were about love, loss, fear, innocence, strength. The real God was Imagination. I was Muslim but fiction was my true religion.

The God of Imagination lived in fairytales. And the best fairytales made you fall in love. It was while flicking through *Sleeping Beauty* that I met my first love. Ivar. He was a six-year-old bello ragazzo with blond hair and eyebrows. He had bomb-blue eyes and his two front teeth were missing.

The road to Happily Ever After, however, was paved with political barbed wire. Three things stood in my way.

1. The object of my affection didn't know he was the object of my affection.
2. The object of my affection preferred Action Man to Princess Aurora.
3. The object of my affection was a boy and I wasn't allowed to love a boy.

But I was allowed to dream. And in my dreams Ivar became my prince, hacking at the thorns that hemmed me in. He slew dragons, fought fire with a shield and sword, all to a Tchaikovsky score. The boy was Michael Jackson bad. And he would kiss me to break the spell. He would kiss me but all that'd break would be my heart. He could never be mine.

While Ivar roamed my dreams, my parents' nightmares were re-enacted on CNN. The TV flooded our lives with bad news about Somalia. Young gabdo were raped and mutilated, an old man was tortured with teeth-extraction by pliers until he bled to death. I worried about my grandfather and grandmother, who were still in Somalia. I knew Ayeeyo would survive: she was strong and inventive. Awoowe, however, was senile and couldn't tell a gun-clip from a gumball. Every day I asked Hooyo, 'When're we heading home?'

'Soon,' she'd sigh, 'soon.'

'You said that yesterday.'

'It's up to God, son.'

'Maybe God doesn't know best.'

She slapped me for blaspheming but I wouldn't let it go: 'God is punishing our people.'

Hooyo pulled me close. 'No, son, we're punishing each other.'

She pressed me against her basketball-shaped belly. She smelt of barafuun and cocoa butter, of milk and memories. Hooyo smelt of home.

Our home smelt of fear that even foox couldn't conceal. We lived too close to Kilimani Police Station. My waalid may have reinvented themselves but to the booliis we were still refugee bastards who sucked on Nanny State's iron teats until there was nothing left for her legitimate children. The irony was that Nanny State's teats were drier than my dad's Donny Osmond cassettes. That shosho's nutrients had long been sapped by Moi's regime. But that only worsened the trickle of poison, the building animus against Somalis.

Most Somalis lived in Eastleigh, a slum that made Soweto seem dope, but despite the filth and farabutos, business was booming there to the tune of $30 million a month. These Somalis were financial sorcerers. Illegal-immigrant financial-sorcerers. The police devised a Plan of Action. Armed with AK47s, they began a walalo witch-hunt. You could be at work or working your honey, your ass was under arrest.

The cops weren't cruel. They gave options: 'Kipanda,' 'Kitu kidogo' or 'Kakuma.' Most folks didn't have kipandas to live in Kenya so they paid kitu kidogo. Kakuma wasn't an option. One of the largest African refugee camps, it was also known as Never-Never Land: meaning, 'If you end up there, you'll never-never be allowed to leave.'

My parents weren't down with that Plan of Action, so they devised their own.

'Never open the gates to the police,' Aabo told Waithaka, our watchman.

'Never tell them that Somalis live here,' Hooyo told Mary, the maid.

'You're not allowed to play outside,' they told us.

The booliis became the bogeymen of our nightmares. At night every sound was sinister: dogs barking as iron gates creaked, owls hooting. Aziza and I shared a bedroom and we shuddered under our blankets.

'What if they snatch us?' asked Azi, who was only five years old.

'They won't,' I said uncertainly.

'But what if?'

'Insha Allah, they won't.'

'Will you protect me?'

'Yes.'

'Promise?'

'I promise.'

'Cross you heart and hope to die.'

'We're Muslim. We say, 'wallahi billahi tallahi.''

'Say it then.'

'Wallahi billahi tallahi.'

'Can I share your bed?'

'No.'

'Fadlan.'

'No. You'll wet the bed.'

'I'm wearing a nappy.'

I considered this. After some thought I scooted over and she scrambled in next to me. We lay in the dark, ears pricked up for eerie sounds.
'Xirsi?'
'What?'
'Tell me a story.'

'Once upon a time in Lavington there lived a chica named Kohl Black. She was plumpness personified: thick thighs, lips, Afro. Her eyes were the colour of coffee. Her skin was darker than liquorice. Kohl was supuu but her stepmother Immaculate considered her subhuman, 'a walking, talking whale.' Immaculate, as her name suggested, was obsessive. She obsessed about her size and skin-tone, about her home and hygiene. She bathed in milk even though there were shortages around the country. She nourished her skin with eggs, avocado and bleach. She wore shoulder-padded blouses and wigs made from the finest horsehair. Immaculate was a dem that made Princess Diana look pedestrian.

'Every week a herbal doctor came to cure her 'ailments', which ranged from disputes with her dead husband's relatives, who insisted that she killed him (a claim she always denied), to fights with fanya-kazis who accused her of being an abusive employer (again, a claim she denied, although she relished whupping her maid Purity's ass).

'The daktari's diagnosis was simple: 'Envylitis.' Anyone who wished Immaculate ill suffered from this sickness. So he prescribed 'medicine'. Her dead husband's relatives soon took their kelele elsewhere and Purity put a stop to her nonsense (although Immaculate still enjoyed klepping her).

'The doctor didn't tell Immaculate that she too suffered from 'Envylitis'. Immaculate always asked, 'Daktari, daktari, who's the finest of them all?'

'The doctor had sense. 'Ni wewe tu. You, madam, are the finest of them all.' If he didn't say so, Immaculate would hire snipers to take out her competition, thereby diminishing his client base.

'One day, while Immaculate and her doctor were sipping tea, Kohl sashayed into the sitting room. She wore a tight kanga. The doctor nearly spilled his tea. After grabbing her textbooks, Kohl sauntered out.

"Haki, I'm housing a small elephant,' sighed Immaculate. 'That girl eats her body weight in githeri. No wonder our fanya-kazis are so malnourished: she eats all their food!'

"That girl is bodacious,' said the doctor. 'Fullness is fineness.'

"Ati?' snapped Immaculate. 'You mean to tell me Kohl is the finest of them all?'

"Err...' the doctor started sweating. 'No, of course not.'

'But Immaculate knew the truth.

"Then it is your job to remove her. Otherwise all the juju in the world won't save you.'

"Sawa sawa.'

'But the doctor didn't comply. On his way out he saw Kohl reading on the veranda and warned her.

"Ngai,' said Kohl, 'I knew that mama was insane but not Mathari-asylum insane. What should I do, daktari?'

"Kimbia to Kawangware. She'll never find you there.'

'So Kohl ran to Kawangware. Clad in only a kanga and a pair of slippers, she felt underprepared. As she entered the slum she closed her nose. Sewage flowed everywhere. Flies buzzed around piles of faeces. An mtoto had stuck flowers in some manure - '

'Miss Mumbi! Miss Mumbi, please come to my office.'

Miss Edna, the English principal, cut Miss Mumbi's story short. We were so jazzed by the fairytale that we all cried, 'Aww!'

'Worry not, watoto,' said Miss Mumbi as Miss Edna

escorted her out, 'I shall finish the story of Kohl Black and the Seven Street Boys.'

The class cheered, but all I could hear was Miss Edna hissing, 'Not if I've anything to do with it.'

Ivar came over to me and said, 'My mum complained about Miss Mumbi.'

I didn't tell him that Hooyo had also complained about her.

'She's supposed to teach you Ingriis not Kenyati,' Hooyo had said. So she started schooling me herself. Every day I developed my vocabulary. Initially, the words felt wooden but now I could string sentences together.

'Why your mum complain?' I asked Ivar.

'She said Miss Mumbi is a bad teacher.'

'Why?' I wanted him to keep talking. His breath smelt like a baby's.

'She's just not good.'

His hair looked better than Aziza's Barbie: so fly.

'I didn't like Miss Mumbi's story,' he whispered.

'It's good story.'

'No, it's terrible. She made Snow White black.'

'So?'

'Everyone knows Snow White isn't black.'

Suddenly Ivar wasn't so fly. I thought Miss Mumbi's retelling was excellent – crazy but excellent. I told Ivar this. He stared at me and said something that made me want to cry.

'Are you a refugee?'

I wanted my refugee status revoked. Sharci la'aan meant a life of shame.

The Kenyan police thought so too. Our shame was their salary on the side. That afternoon they crept into our compound. Waithaka, our watchman, had gone to the kiosk but he wouldn't have been able to stop them.

Mary was eating matoke on the veranda when she

spotted them. She ran inside and warned us.

'Ngai, mama, the police are outside.'

Without missing a beat Hooyo rushed us into her bedroom. The doorbell rang.

'Mary, don't let them in and don't tell them we live here.'

'Haya, mama.'

Hooyo shoved us into her dressing-room and locked the door. My parent's dressing-room smelled of unsi and Ungaro. Aziza and I sometimes applied Hooyo's lipstick and kissed the mirror. We now crouched on the floor and called out to God.

'Uskut!' hissed Hooyo. 'Now's not the time!' Then she pressed her belly and groaned.

'What's wrong, Hooyo?' asked Aziza.

'Nothing, sweetie.' Hooyo breathed heavily.

'Is the baby coming?' I asked.

Hooyo didn't answer, just gestured me to be quiet. Sweat soaked her forehead.

We could hear Mary arguing with the booliis but we couldn't make out what was being said. Hooyo started hyperventilating. The spot we were sitting on became wet.

'Akh! Aziza, why'd you pee?'

'It's Hooyo.'

She was right: Hooyo had urinated on the floor. I felt sick with fear.

'My waters broke,' she said.

'What does that mean?'

'The baby's coming.' Hooyo looked ready to scream. I stuffed Aabo's socks into her mouth.

'Bite on that,' I said.

Aziza started crying.

'Uskut!' I said. 'Hooyo needs us.'

We heard someone in the bedroom. We held our breaths. The handle on the dressing-room door turned. A knock came. I moved round in front of Hooyo and Aziza to try and shield them.

'Mama,' came Mary's voice, 'the police have gone.'

We didn't believe her. She rattled at the handle again. 'Haki, they've gone.'

'Cross your heart and hope to die,' I said.

'Wallahi billahi tallahi.'

I opened the door. Mary rushed to remove the socks from Hooyo's mouth. 'Mama, come to the bed. The police have gone.'

'Mary, what happen Hooyo?' whimpered Aziza.

'She'll be sawa.' Mary supported Hooyo to the bed. 'Xirsi, go call dad.'

'I help Hooyo.'

'You can help by calling your dad,' Mary said, shooing me out and closing the door.

I scurried to the sitting-room and dialled Aabo's office.

'I'm on my way,' he said.

'Hurry, Aabo, hurry!'

The baby was born in Hooyo's bedroom. A girl. In honour of the midwife who delivered her, Hooyo named my new sister Maryam.

'Why not just call her Mary?' I asked.

'Because we're Muslim,' hissed Hooyo. 'In Islam Mary is Maryam.'

We all crowded around the bambino. She had feathery hair, a tiny nose and Hooyo's full lips. She was bella.

When Aabo arrived the first thing he did was give Mary a pay-rise. The second thing was sack Waithaka for not watching over us. The final thing was hug Hooyo.

I looked at my family and recalled the scene in Bambi when the baby was born. If that scene were re-enacted Hooyo would be the doe, Maryam Bambi, and Aziza Thumper. Aabo, Mary and I would be the forest critters leading the celebrations.

Aabo was still celebrating on my final day of kindergarten. He cranked Sade on the car stereo as we drove to Pine Tree. As he sang along to *The Sweetest Taboo* I spotted the chokoras outside Studio House. The street-boy who once pointed his middle finger at me now stuck his tongue out. I shrugged as we drove past.

As we turned into Kindaruma Road I feared the baboons would terrorise us. But we didn't see them. For now.

To commemorate the end of term the teachers threw a party for the pre-schoolers. We donned hats and drank Sunny Delight. There had been no more political Story Time sessions since Miss Mumbi was sacked three weeks ago: we'd had to contend with Miss Consolata's stodgy sheeko. I missed Miss Mumbi's hauteur, her sense of high drama and obsession with decolonisation. Next term I would begin at S^t. Austin's Academy, a private school in Lavington. Aabo had enrolled me in the fifth grade, but with my faulty English I feared failure. I would miss the kindergarten and the sense of arrested development it afforded me.

After the party Ivar came up to me and apologised for calling me a refugee.

'Hirsi,' he asked, 'what does 'refugee' mean?'

'It mean no home, fighting, death.'

'Have you ever seen a dead body?'

'Yes.'

'Cool!'

He seemed excited by this, so I told him gory stories galore.

'And you saw all that?' he asked.

'Yes, I see all.'

'Did your mummy protect you?'

'My mummy and my daddy.'

'Would you go back to Somalia?'

'I want very badly but Somalia no good. Fighting all time.'

'You can stay here now.'

'I will.'

'Hirsi, will you be my best friend?'

'I promise.'

'Cross your heart and hope to die.'

'I'm Muslim. I say 'wallahi billahi tallahi'.'

Afterwards, while the other kids were playing indoors, Ivar and I snuck off to ride the swings. We took turns in pushing one another. Every time he pushed me I squealed and swung back. That was the happiest moment of my life. But it was short-lived.

'I want to climb the trees,' said Ivar.

'Ivar, I afraid of monkeys.'

'Don't be a scaredy-cat. It'll be fun.'

That didn't reassure me. But I wanted to please him so I acquiesced. There was a large pine tree at the back of the kindergarten. We went over to it and Ivar said, 'Hoist me up.'

I took hold of his legs and lifted him. He was strong for a six-year old and pulled himself up onto the first branch.

'Okay, Ivar. Time to come down. Miss Consolata be very angry.'

'I don't care,' he said, swinging from one branch to the next. I was so scared he'd fall that I shut my eyes.

'Look, Hirsi. Can you do this?' He hung from a branch using one arm.

'Ivar, please don't –'

As soon as he said, 'I'm climbing higher,' I heard the familiar, 'OoOoAhAh.' Like a bad dream, a baboon swung onto the tree. Ivar was too high up to hepa.

'I get help,' I called, but Ivar didn't want me to go.

'Please don't leave me!' he cried.

The baboon screeched as it made its way to Ivar's branch. I knew it would kill him so I shouted, 'Jump, Ivar. Jump, I catch you.'

But Ivar was petrified. He refused to let go and the baboon was gaining on him.

'Will you catch me?' he asked, through tears.

'I promise.'

'Say wallahi billahi tallahi.'

'Wallahi – '

The baboon leapt at Ivar, who let go of the branch. I tried to catch him but he hit the ground head-first and I heard bones break. His angles were like a pretzel. His eyes were open and blood oozed from his mouth like drool. He was Sleeping Beauty and I was the prince who had to save him. So I pressed my lips against his and kissed him. I kissed him until I tasted his blood.

'Ivar, please wake up,' I moaned. But this wasn't *Sleeping Beauty* with its Happily-Ever-After. It wasn't even *Kohl Black and the Seven Street Boys*, a story with a beginning and no ending. None of the fairytales I had read had prepared me for this.

I looked up and the whole school had gathered in the playground. All the kids were crying and Miss Edna rushed off to call the ambulance. Miss Consolata took me to the outside tap to clean up.

'Me get deported?' I asked, tears streaming down my face.

'No,' she said, although her tone suggested otherwise.

What if I was deported? What would happen to my family? I began to vomit. Miss Consolata said something but all I could hear was the baboon screeching in the trees. I couldn't tell whether it was hungry or in heat, or whether it was mocking me, laughing at the monkey on my back.

SHOGA

My grandmother worked my roots with the vigour of a woman who meant business. She dug her fingernails into my 'fro and when she discovered dandruff she pulled out her clippers and said, 'Waryaa, fix up! Hadiikale, I shall shave you cleaner than a baby's ass.'

'Ayeeyo, I want to be braided not be given a bloody sermon.'

'Hododo!' she clapped her hands. 'You've mastered the art of backchat. Now learn the basics of hygiene.'

'Ayeeyo, man!'

'Is it not true? And furthermore, this business of me braiding your hair has to stop! You're a boy not a lady-boy!'

'You know you love me,' I smiled. 'Besides, what's wrong with being a lady-boy? It's a good look.'

She pulled my hair and said, 'Waryaa, if you grow up to be gay, walaahi I will do saar.'

'Saar' was a brand of Somali exorcism. Those 'possessed' – which was code for the mentally unstable – were put through their paces. Healers would beat drums to release spirits from the possessed, who would shimmy and shake and, if they got too frisky, would face the kind of beat-down usually reserved for criminals. Such superstition has always been rife in the bush and my gran, a country gal through and through, knew its effectiveness at deterring unacceptable behaviour.

I smiled as she flexed my follicles. My grandmother did not know that I was gay. I've always loved being gay. Sure, Kenya was not exactly Queer Nation but my sexuality gave me joy. I was young, not so dumb and full of cum! There was no place for me in heaven but I was content munching devil's pie here on earth.

I was seventeen and I specialised in two things: weed and sex. And there was only one person in my neighbourhood who served both those dishes on a steaming plate for me.

Boniface.

But I've missed a beat, my bambinos. A narrative without a back-story is like meat with no bone; there's no juice to it. So let me take two steps back.

My family moved to Kenya in '91, after my dad hauled our asses from Mogadishu. I don't remember much about Somalia – I was only a toddler when we fled – but over the years Mogadishu assumed mythical status in our lives. It could only truly flourish in selective memory. It was years later that I learnt the precise term for what my family and millions of other Somalis had experienced during the war: post-traumatic stress.

But my father was not one for wasting time. He got to work and started amassing a small fortune by selling blankets and medicine to NGOs headed for Mogadishu. My mum did her bit and became a pharmacist in Hurlingham. Whilst baba na mama made money, my gran took care of home.

All that changed in '94. My parents were driving home from Trattoria Restaurant one night when they got stopped by the police. The cops ordered them to get out of the car but my dad refused. Kenyan police are the shiftiest crooks this side of the Sahara. If they want to extort you, nobody can stop them. If they want to make you disappear, no one can prevent it. My father knew this so he refused to get out. Without missing a beat, the police fired three shots in his head. Then they blasted my mother's brains out when she started screaming. Their bodies were found floating in Athi River the next day. I was seven years old.

Whilst my gran's peers were settling quietly into old age she now had to support both of us. We owned our small maisonette so housing wasn't an issue. My parents had taken out life insurance but it wasn't enough for us to live on. My grandmother took half the cash and invested it in a small import-export business she ran out of our living-room. The rest went into my education.

As the years passed gran decided she needed help around the house. She found it difficult to bend over and clean floors and cook three meals a day, raise a teenager *and* run a business. She didn't want another woman in her home. She wanted a man who was strong enough to cook, clean and carry water to the tank. She wanted a man to protect us from burglars. Basically she wanted a budget superhero.

Enter Boniface.

Boniface was from Burundi and my grandma dug this. She dug the fact that he was a refugee like us but I was more impressed with his muscle mass. While she saw enough brawn to carry three sacks of bariis at once, I saw prime beefcake. Papi was beautiful and he looked like he was packing. I licked my lips and locked and loaded.

Every day I'd go to my window and watch him wash clothes outside. When it became humid he'd remove his shirt, fold it and place it on the ground. His pectorals would be slick with sweat. Whenever he saw me, he'd smile and wink. I'd stick my tongue out. He'd make a fist and pretend to punch himself. I'd flip him the finger.

'I'll tell ayeeyo!' His eyes glinted.

'Tell her,' I laughed.

'She shall thup you,' he warned.

'And I shall thup *you*!'

'Bring it!' he said, flexing his muscles.

'Ever tasted the flying fist of Judah?' I asked.

'More like the flying fist of foolishness!'

'Are you challenging me?'

'I believe I am,' he said.

'Then it's on. Tonight. Backyard.'

He laughed. 'We shall see who thups who.'

We sneaked into the backyard that evening. My grandmother was asleep so we tried to keep it quiet.

All I wanted was to feel his body against mine and if it took a wrestling match to achieve this, I was game. I thought he'd go easy on me but he lifted me up like a ragdoll, ready for a literal smackdown.

'Put me down!' I yelled, wriggling in his arms.

'What do you say?'

'Fuck you!'

'Now, now,' he said, tightening his grip. 'I'll let you down on one condition.'

'No dice!'

'Are you sure?' he asked, 'It involves a treat.'

My ears pricked up. 'What kind of treat?'

He put me down and reached into his pocket. He removed a spliff – purple haze. I eyed it greedily.

'I never smoke alone,' he said. 'So I was wondering – '

'Yes!' I said, quickly. 'I'll puff with you.'

'But if ayeeyo busts us you take the blame.'

'Toka!' I scoffed.

'I know you want some,' he dangled the spliff.

I wiped my drool and said, 'It's a deal. But I get to light it!'

We went to his quarters and smoked up. Boniface's room used to be a storage space but he'd transformed it with paint and posters. There was a cassette player and a stack of bootleg tapes on the bedside table. The cassettes were by artists like Koffi Olomide and Papa Wemba.

'Don't you have any hip-hop?' I asked.

'Hip-hop is shit,' he said. 'Check this out.' He pulled out a cassette, opened the tape-recorder and slid it in. He then sprawled on the bed and passed me the joint.

The weed hit me the moment the music started playing. It was an old soul record. The singer sang in a tone that made me feel slinky. I got up and snaked my hips. Boniface looked on. He smiled and stroked his chest. I walked over and lay next to him. He didn't inch away. Instead he examined my face, ran his calloused palm across my cheek. I noticed a beauty spot under his right eye. I touched it. His skin was soft.

I placed the joint on a nearby ashtray. I pulled my tee-shirt over my head and slid out of my shorts. He kissed me, tongue tasting of weed. He broke the kiss to unbutton his shirt. His abdomen was cut like slabs of chocolate. He removed his trousers and wasn't wearing underwear. His thighs were thick, dick hard. I bent down and deep-throated him. He smelt of soap. He pushed his hips back and forth. I stopped to come up for air. He helped me out of my underwear and spread my limbs, licked every inch of me until I was sex-funky. He then reached for the joint and took a long pull. He blew the smoke in my mouth. I was open.

That night we fucked until the bed threatened to collapse. After we came we went into the kitchen and made Spanish omelettes and tea. We wolfed the food down and went back to his room to smoke some more.

As we puff-puff-passed, I considered what had happened. Sure, I'd fooled around with boys before but this was different. Boniface was a man who fucked like he ate: greedily. I relished the thought of him feasting on me again. I went to bed dreaming of bubbles that would never burst.

After school the next day I ran inside the house to find Boniface making dinner. Ayeeyo was in the kitchen, smoking sheesha.

'What's this haraka business?' she asked. 'Usually, I have to drag you in by force. What gives?'

'I just wanted to see you,' I kissed her.

She gave me a look that said, 'Wacha mchezo.' She continued filling up the kitchen with smoke. Boniface glanced at me and I smiled. Ayeeyo noticed but said nothing.

'Boniface, serve this boy his dinner. He needs to do his homework.'

'Yes, mama,' said Boniface. He piled pasta onto my plate. He was wearing tight shorts and a Beasties tee. As I admired his legs my grandmother watched me. She kept quiet. Boniface poured sauce on my pasta and gave me the plate. I sat on the veranda and waited for Ayeeyo to leave the kitchen.

She didn't leave until midnight. By then I had given up and gone to bed. Boniface had also retired to his room. I could hear Ayeeyo playing Ludo alone, dice clacking against board. I knew she was afraid to go to sleep, afraid of being haunted by nightmares. She had clung onto my parents because they were all she had. It was years after their deaths before she finally accepted her loss. I had come to take their place. She was afraid that once I left home for college I too would never return. I tried consoling her but she didn't want pity. She wanted a guarantee. I couldn't give her that.

Eventually the dice stopped rolling and she went to sleep. That's when I heard a tap on my window. I jumped up and opened the curtains. Boniface was outside, grinning. I told him I'd meet him in his room. When I got there, he was sprawled naked on his bed, puffing a joint. I bent down, kept his dick wet. He pulled me up, laid me on my back. I unbuttoned my shirt, loosened my belt. He opened me up using lips, fingertips, tongue-tricks. He grabbed some Vaseline, slipped on a condom and fucked me until I was sticky with sweat. After we came we wiped ourselves clean and continued smoking.

'Boniface,' I said, 'what do you dream about?'

'Leaving Kenya,' he replied.

'Where would you go?'

'Somewhere exotic like England.'

'But what would you do there?' I asked.

'I'd become an engineer. That's what I studied in Burundi. I could use that degree.'

'You have a degree?' I asked.

'Yah man, I did three years in college before the war began,' he said.

I imagined Boniface as an academic. He'd do well in England.

'Na wewe?' he asked. 'What do you dream of?'

'Love,' I replied.

'But you *are* loved,' he said. 'By your grandmother, by me – '

'You don't love me!' I smiled.

'Haki! Otherwise I wouldn't be thinking of you kila siku.'

I played the coquette. 'Hata mimi nakupenda.'

'Course you do!' he grinned. 'It's hard not to!'

I punched him lightly. He hugged me tight. I left his quarters high on happiness and heat. As I tiptoed to my room I noticed that Ayeeyo's light was switched on, her door slightly ajar. I went to bed, praying that she didn't know what had happened.

I woke up the next morning to find Ayeeyo making breakfast. I greeted her but she didn't reply.

'Where's Boniface?' I asked. 'He usually makes breakfast.'

Ayeeyo didn't look at me. She silently added pepper and tomatoes to the eggs in the frying pan. When she finished cooking she turned off the stove, slopped the eggs onto my plate and said, 'Eat up. Your bus will be here soon.'

Her voice dripped with contempt. I knew better than to say anything, so I took the plate and ate the eggs. Ayeeyo waited for me to finish. When I was done, she gave me a napkin and told me to go.

'Ayeeyo – ' I began.

'You'll miss your bus,' she said.

I grabbed my backpack and left the house. I couldn't concentrate at school that day. I was petrified that Ayeeyo had discovered my affair with Boniface. What would she do? Had she fired him? Would she kick me out of the house? By the time I returned home that afternoon I was a wreck.

I walked into the kitchen to find Ayeeyo cooking dinner. I was afraid to ask the obvious but I had to know.

'Where's Boniface?' I said.

'He's not here,' she replied chirpily.

'You sound happy about that.'

'Of course I am. The man was a thief!'

'What did he steal?' I asked.

'Something that can't be replaced,' was her reply.

'Like what?'

'Does it matter?' she snapped. 'The fact is the man is a thief and I don't tolerate thieves in my house. Or drug addicts for that matter.'

'Boniface is not a drug addict! What the hell are you talking about?'

She looked at me and smirked, 'Then why were the two of you smoking weed in his room last night? And the night before?'

My stomach dropped. 'We weren't smoking!' I said. 'We were just listening to music.'

'I can forgive a little marijuana but the two of you were doing something else in that room. Something that makes me want to retch!'

I was about to shit a brick but I kept my ass in check. 'Tell me, Ayeeyo, what *were* we doing in his room?'

She steadied herself on the sink, as if literally gagging on the words. 'I will not let a fanya kazi corrupt you. You will *not* become a...a – '

'Go on, Ayeeyo, you can say it,' I snarled. 'I will not become a khaniis? A shoga? A faggot? Well, tough luck! My ass *is* a khaniis. I am a shoga, a faggot.'

She smacked me so hard across the face that I lost my balance and fell onto the ground. I got up and said, 'I will leave this house one day and you will die a lonely, embittered old woman.'

She looked like she had been punched. Her eyes welled up but she wouldn't allow me to see tears. So she left the kitchen and went to her bedroom. She didn't come out for four days.

My relationship with my grandmother was never the same again. She stopped speaking to me altogether and we became two strangers bound by blood and bad history. When I finished high school she didn't show up to my graduation ceremony. When I got a scholarship to Central Saint Martins in England she didn't congratulate me. On the day I was leaving for London she didn't wish me luck. She didn't whisper comforting words or urge me to come home soon. I got on that plane with a suitcase of painful memories and little else.

I called Ayeeyo regularly from London but she never picked up the phone. I began to be afraid that something might have happened to her. I called Nairobi every day for four years and there was never a response. One day I called and a woman picked up. I jumped with excitement.

'Hi, I'm looking for my grandmother,' I said. 'Is she home?'

'I'm really sorry, son,' the woman said. 'Your grandmother passed away a week ago but we only found her body last night. She's been taken to the morgue. I was her nurse.'

The air felt like it had been sucked out of the room. I sat down on the ground and breathed slowly. 'How did she die?' I asked.

'She had a stroke. I'm really sorry.'

'But you were her nurse!' I shouted. 'Where were you?'

'Your grandmother told me to take the week off.'

'Are you serious?' I screamed. 'You left a sick eighty-year-old woman by herself?'

'I'm sorry.'

I wanted to strangle her but was more livid with myself. I was the one who had hurt my grandmother. I was the one who had abandoned her. She had died alone and it broke my heart. After I spoke to the nurse I contacted some relatives in Kenya and asked them if they would bury her. In Islam the funeral has to happen immediately after the person's death. I wired my savings to my relatives and they buried my grandmother that afternoon.

The next few months were spent in a self-destructive haze of alcohol and weed. I skipped classes, missed assignments and almost got expelled. I took a leave of absence from college and got a job as a bartender in a dingy club in Soho. It was there that I met Ignacio, a Colombian émigré who taught me to how to make caipirinhas. We spent every evening after work in his bedsit, sipping cocktails and sucking cock.

One night Ignacio played an old school soul record that made my heart skip a beat. It was a melody from another time and place. It was the song that Boniface played for me when we first made love.

'What's this tune called?' I asked Ignacio.

'*All I Do*,' he replied, lighting up a joint. 'Stevie Wonder.'

I took the joint from him, lay down on the bed and opened my legs wide. Ignacio smiled. As he fucked me I closed my eyes and imagined Boniface in his place, working me, tightening me like a knot before giving me release. I imagined Ayeeyo in her grave in Nairobi. I imagined my mother and my father. I imagined our modest home in Nairobi: the baobab and jacaranda trees in the backyard, the quiet veranda at the front. My whole life zigged and zagged in my head. When I came, I cried. Ignacio asked me why.

I didn't tell him about my loss. Instead, I said, 'Insha Allah, everything will work out.' He looked at me quizzically. But I kept repeating this statement louder and louder until it created an incantatory effect. I repeated this statement until it became something I could hold onto, something I could believe in; until it shifted from mantra to fact.

IF I WERE A DANCE

woy had *moves*. Toes tightened into corkscrews. He fucked with his body's limits, bending, flexing until he broke through. Attitude and Arabesque became pop, lock, drop. No sweat.

Such control is dangerous.

I know this dance.

It is ours.

C'est énigmatique? Hakuna shida. It's a strange story but I'll share it.

The man up there is Narciso but I prefer to call him Narcissus. If his ego were bottled a drop would poison a scorpion. I lived with this man for three years; I can handle him for three more nights.

When we were together we wrote a performance piece called 'Dance of The Fairies' that charted our romance from its inception to what we only belatedly realised was its demise. There were bits of dialogue – poetic – but mostly it was about body language. Our affair was primal: between fights we fucked, between fucks we fought. But we were both artists: we distilled our drama into dance. The eventual piece, however, was five hours long, and we never actually performed it.

After we broke up I met a theatre producer. I was striking a pose at a schmooze-fest when I pitched my idea to her. She thought I was on bootleg smack. Nevertheless, she gave me her card, hoping she'd never see me again. I sent her my showreel the next morning, and harassed her for months to watch it. Eventually she did, and to her own surprise liked what she saw. She proposed a three-night run. She would find the venue, cut a deal with the management. She wouldn't pay for costumes or set but I insisted she pay us. Our salaries were below scale – which beats no-scale.

The only snag in my hustle was Madam: I'd created the piece with Narciso and couldn't perform it without his say-so. So I went to see him.

'I'm over it,' he said, smoking. 'That shit is so two-thousand-and-late. You need to keep it moving.'

I looked around his bedsit. The mattress was stained. The laptop had a film of dust on it; next to it was a jumbo-sized bottle of lube.

'Single life suits you,' I said, sizing up a crusty tissue discarded on the tatty carpet.

'I'm helping Mr. Kleenex's kids through college,' he replied. 'How much are these punks paying?'

'Below scale.'

'Do I look like Oliver Twist's Angolan brother? Tell this mama she needs to pay. Below scale!' He laughed at the idea.

'Mr. Kleenex's kids are doing swell,' I said. 'You've used so much of his product for your wankertorium sessions that his *great*-grandchildren will be doing swell. We, on the other hand, are piss-poor artists. Let's do our ting.'

'And what exactly is our ting, Anas?' Narciso cocked his eyebrow. 'Gato, get off my goddam dick and go ride someone else's!'

I started making my exit. 'Don't slam the door behind you,' he said, reaching for the bottle of lube. 'I don't want you fucking up my concentration!'

'Concentrate on this,' I said. 'If you don't show up at my flat for rehearsal tomorrow at exactly 5.30 pm I'll have your replacement in by six.' I slammed the door behind me.

It was a gamble: Narciso was capable of putting pride ahead of paying his bills. However he did show up, albeit at 5.45. We got to work and devised a plan. We broke the segments down into three acts, which would be performed individually over three nights. The first act, 'This Is How I Love You,' would chronicle the first blissful year of our relationship. The second, 'If I Were A Dance,' would chronicle the period when the fun screeched to a halt. The final act, 'The World Has Made Me The Man Of My Dreams,' would re-enact our break-up.

'I will agree to this plan on one condition,' said Narciso.

'Shoot.'

'If we perform this piece, that's it. We're done. I have my own life now and you have yours. No more coming round to my yard arksing me whether I've gone to work, whether I have food in the house, whether I've done my laundry. If we do this performance, we take the monyeta and disperse our separate ways. Clear?'

I bit my lip and said, 'Crystal.'

'Good. Now, let's get this bad boy on the road.'

We decided on the set-list for each night: Meshell Ndegeocello for the first act, Amel Larrieux for the second and Sade for the third. We selected songs from each artist's catalogue, found a rehearsal space, and put our backs into it.

The first session was a mess. We kept fluffing our counts: each dip and glide was out. But by the third our bodies became familiar to each other again. His chest felt warm against mine. His musk, the intensity of his gaze, his sandpapery palms against my soft neck, his sweat on my collarbone. Everything about him felt right.

After each song we broke apart awkwardly.

But this was no exercise in sentimentality. My rent was overdue and my shifts at the call-centre weren't cutting the cake. I needed this to work on a monetary level.

By the seventh rehearsal we had our routine down. The core elements were tightly choreographed but the details would be improvised. We plotted the arc, and how each evening's storyline would begin and end. We would fill in the blanks on impulse and bounce off of each other.

Then it came down to logistics. We cajoled our friends to chip in gratis and soon we had people to do lighting, sound and design. We made our own costumes. It was time to rock it.

This Is How I Love You

Word got out about our project, and the mutual friends who had witnessed our personal drama firsthand quickly snapped up all the seats in the small venue our producer had found, though she stopped us giving them the comps many of them felt they deserved.

'Are you ready?' I asked Narciso as we prepared to go on-stage on the opening night.

He swigged back his Tanqueray and said, 'Bring the heat.'

The house-lights dimmed. Meshell Ndegeocello's *Leviticus: Faggot* began to play. The bassline and snare snaked round me. I strutted onto the stage, bopping my head. I was wearing an Afro wig, so there was bounce in my hair, hips *and* hiny. I did a semi-split, held my stance, made the booty clap. My fingers clicked to the chords. The lights turned mango-red. I lowered my split, synchronised it to the snare. Fingers clicked, booty clapped. I then slid up, breakdance-style, to cries of 'Whoops! There it is!' from the audience.

As I was catching flow Narciso came through. *Levitus: Faggot* segued into *Let Me Have You*. Narciso prowled half en pointe, pressed his body against mine. He dipped it low, crunked his way up, abdominals on a serpentine tip. I caught his breath. Tanqueray.

I pushed him away. The music stopped.

'What's the matter?' he said. 'Don't you like me?'

'No,' I said.

He smiled. 'I'm sure we can remedy that.'

'How so?'

'Like this.' He kissed me. A girl in the audience wolf-whistled.

'You're going to have to come better,' I said.

'Like this, maybe?' He traced his palm across my neck. His touch felt necessary but I had to maintain.

'I need to know more about you. What's your stylistix?'

'Place of birth: Angola. Date of birth: 21st of May. Country of residence: England. Man I want to be with: you.'

The audience laughed and whistled.

I smiled. 'Place of birth: Somalia. Date of birth: 5th of October. Country of residence: England. Man I want to be with: undecided!'

This drew even bigger applause. 'Tell him, Anas!' shouted one of my friends.

'Tell you what,' said Narciso. 'You'll make up your mind by the end of the night.'

'Bring it!' I said.

Ndegeocello's *Beautiful* started playing. Narciso grabbed my hand and led me into a waltz. As we danced to screened images of the Southbank I remembered the abandon I felt when we first met. The background image shifted to a shot of Narciso's bedroom, tidied for the occasion. The lights went down but the song kept playing. We rushed backstage for a quick costume change. We didn't look at each other.

It was time for the final scene of tonight's act.

Narciso's body was draped in red silk, mine in ochre. I touched his torso, pulled him close. I kissed his cheek,

licked his lobe. The silk slipped off. We lay together on
the stage wearing Speedos. As the heat intensified, conga
drums kicked in. We panted in synch. The music stopped.
We stared at each other and I saw years. I saw melancholy and yearning and resentment cross his face. I
looked away.

As we lay together in silence the seasons changed on
the screen behind us. I gathered myself as Meshell
Ndegeocello's *This is How I Love You* echoed around us.
I laughed soundlessly for montage effect but mainly to
mask the fact that I wanted to cry. Narciso sensed this but
played his part too, laughing soundlessly. We lay on the
ground and performed our past as the song faded us out.

If I Were A Dance

Our tendons were tight the next day but it was time for
round two. I was afraid of the revealing nature of this act,
and during the afternoon's rehearsal my face burned
every time Narciso held my hand or hips. I wanted to
trace his lips, remind him of why we had loved once. But
he didn't want to remember. Instead he performed his
routine like a shadow-boxer intent on punching away
each memory until he had sweated me out. By the end of
the rehearsal the room stunk of Tanqueray and smoke
and body odour.

I took a swig of Narciso's drink and shook out my
limbs. It was time to kick it.

The lights dimmed. Narciso and I walked onto the
stage. I stole a glance at the audience: it was a packed
house. My friends. Ours. His. Strangers. On the screen
behind us was a shot of my kitchen subtitled 'A Year
Later.' I mimed making eggs. The sound effects sizzled.
Narciso leant in close and embraced me from behind. I
closed my eyes and smiled. He felt warm and I felt
needed.

'Baby, I gotta go sort out some shit,' he said, breaking the embrace and heading for the door.

'Can't it wait?' I asked. 'I'm making breakfast.'

He kissed me on my neck and said, 'I'll be back in a jiffy.'

I tossed my imaginary pan of eggs onto the floor and a clanging sound effect echoed all over the theatre.

'If I were a dance, you'd fucking dance me well!' I said. He leant in and kissed me.

'You are a dance and I do know how to dance you.'

Amel Larreaux's *If I Were a Bell*, a dreamy jazz standard, began to play. Narciso stretched his arms wide, shaman-stylo. He glided across the floor, dipping low as if catching deep strokes. The song segued into a Middle-Eastern riddim. Rude bwoy turned dervish like he had hot sand between his toes.

Slide guitars, strobe lights. I watched from the side-line as he worked himself into a hot, sweaty mess. The music stopped.

'See?' he panted. 'I know how to dance you well.'

He grabbed his coat and exited the stage.

I started cleaning up the imaginary spill. As I got my hands dirty a bomb bassline dropped, and I found myself flexing to its funkiness. Scrub-scrub, pop-pop, scrub-scrub, pop. The song was Larrieux's *Sweet Misery*.

The song was about heartbreak and the hip-hop beat salted my wounds. I ground my hips like a skeezer, gyrated until I was sticky-icky. I danced sweat, spittle and dust. I danced even though my toes cramped and my back spasmed. I danced until I cried. This rhythm was all I had left: I couldn't lose it too. When the song ended I collapsed onto the boards. I lay there until the lights went down.

The screen flashed up with the sign '18 Hours Later: 4am'. I heard Narciso yodelling in the background and when the lights came back up he stepped onto the stage, looking drunk.

'Watch this, watch this,' he slurred. 'I know how to dance you really well.' He started stumbling and falling to the ground, getting up and stumbling again. This was no act. I knew he was sloshed. He reeked of whisky. But I kept up my performance. Eventually he collapsed onto the floor and blacked out. I lay next to him and watched his unconscious face.

Amel Larrieux's *Makes Me Whole*, an elegiac love song, filtered through the speakers. It was the song we made love to on our first anniversary. I wiped my face as I stared at him snoring, realising now why we couldn't make it work. The lights went down then up again for the bows. We got a standing ovation that was undoubtedly laced with pity but I didn't care. I took Narciso home, fished his keys from his pocket, placed him in his bed and walked out of his flat and into the night.

The World Has Made Me The Man Of My Dreams

We didn't rehearse the next day. Neither of us could face it: we could barely face each other. We were going to wing it. As we pulled on our costumes and went through our warm-ups before the show Narciso said, 'I'm sorry about last night.'

'No need,' I said tightly.

'You don't have to do this, you know,' he said.

'I want to.'

Body ached, toes mangled, but I had to do this.

'So we're going to re-enact *exactly* what happened?' asked Narciso.

'Yes.'

He sighed. 'Look, I don't want to put you through that shit again.'

'Do your worst.'

As we headed for the stage I started sweating. My feet

were killing me. I could hear the audience clapping. Anxiety coiled itself around my neck, constricted my breathing. Narciso and I stepped onto the stage. The audience cheered us: all old friends now, and witnesses. As we went to first positions I scoped the dusty set, stared up at the lights. The heat was dry. I wanted to melt: drip through the cracks in the floorboards. Narciso twitched without Tanqueray. I scanned the audience for familiar faces.

'Go on Anas!' shouted my pal Paul. 'You can do it!'

That was all I needed to hear.

'Right,' I snarled at Narciso, 'here's your trash.' I tossed an imaginary bag at him. He pretended to catch it although he looked confused.

'Wait a minute,' said Narciso. 'That's not how – '

But I cut him off. 'Narciso, I stayed with you out of pity. Between the fucking around and the just-plain-ole-fuckery you still think you're God's gift to me. Let me break it down for ya. You're a trifling, tanked-up piece of trash and that's what you'll always be. More fool me for trying to change that. You will go back to your hovel and you will hurt. I will never lose sleep over you again.'

'You're being dishonest and insulting!' he hissed.

'You want honesty?' I shouted to the audience. 'This man cheated on me *six* times. He gave me two STIs, stole from me and made me feel cheap.' I turned to Narciso and said, 'How's that for honesty?'

There was a stunned silence. Then Paul shouted again, 'Tell him! The cunt!'

After an awkward pause the woman doing the lighting dimmed the lights. The audience started whispering amongst themselves but mi nah care. I left the stage.

'Where are you going?' shouted Narciso. 'We have a fucking show to finish!'

'As far as I'm concerned,' I shouted back, 'it's finished!'

The theatre, which was small, now seemed like a maze of never-ending corridors, and I got lost trying to find my way out. Finally I saw the exit door and pushed it open. I was greeted by a gust of wind. I shook with relief and started running. I ran even though my feet were bleeding, I ran all the way from Waterloo to Peckham. When I reached my flat, I wrenched off my shoes. My toes were clotted with blood, the nails framed in dark red, and yellow-purple with bruises.

The night wasn't supposed to end like this. Narciso was supposed to break up with me again. He was supposed to call me dull like he had once done. And I was supposed to play the victim. I was supposed to beg him to stay. And as he left me all over again, I was supposed to cry and dance through my tears to Sade's *Stronger Than Pride*.

But I didn't want to beg, I didn't want to cry and I *didn't* want to dance to Sade.

So I didn't.

But I still wanted to dance. I dimmed the lights, swayed in silence. There was no coordination, no fancy footwork, no judgment. I simply swayed, and although a passing siren filled the streets I could still hear my heart. I went where I had to go, where my body and brain took me.

I went where my blood beat.

PAVILION

've been called Queen & Country but my name is Cat. My job is cushty. I don't have to manhandle no-one. I just press the alarm whenever a patient pisses me off and the Nigerian ex-soldiers–turned-nurses do their bit. Animal tranquilisers and whup-ass à la mode are popular treatments. I enjoy watching them with tea and Madeira cake.

But what I really love are the fake names we nurses came up with to mess with patients' heads. I chose Cat Power even though I'm a hard-boiled, six-foot Somali tranny and the real Cat Power is a sensitive white chick with a sultry voice and slight drinking problem. Her name had dragalicious flavour.

My sistren, however, got all spiritual and ting. They called themselves 'Blessing', 'Providence', 'Zipporah'. The patients didn't swallow that mess but they couldn't say shit. One nurse called herself 'Corinthians 13', whilst another one-upped her by calling herself 'The Holy Bible'. 'Cat Power', by contrast, seemed perfectly reasonable.

'Zipporah' ruled the roost. She was a dashiki-wearing earth-woman with soft hands and soulless eyes. She had a babyish voice and she called pliant patients 'My Little Ponies'. Disrespectful ones were dubbed 'My Little Piggies'. 'Little Ponies' were treated to extra servings of slop, cigarettes and sedatives. 'Little Piggies' were manhandled in the corridors, stripped and injected in the ass by Zipporah's goon-squad. After they had been drugged 'Little Piggies' were left lying on the floor. Zippy would pat their heads and smile, 'Rest well.'

She didn't like me. She disliked the idea of a man wearing stockings to work. She disliked my weave, acrylic nails and 'ostentatious spirit.'

'Isn't that too much lipstick, dear?' she smiled one morning.

'You can't have too much of a good thing,' I replied.

'I think you can.'

I reached for my lipgloss and smeared some on. Zippy's smile froze. I strutted down the corridor to catcalls.

'See?' I called out to her. 'You can *never* have too much of a good thing.'

Like all mental clinks, our rules were crazier than our patients. In keeping with our weirdness quota Zipporah had devised a system called 'Five Steps to Paradise'. Modelled on the Seven Heavenly Virtues (charity, chastity etc.), Zipporah's hospital regulations incorporated such gems as:

- Virtue
- Discipline
- Patience
- Temperance
- Reverence

Those who tripped on the stairway to Heaven landed on the 'naughty step'. For staff naughty steps meant less hours, fewer holidays, night shifts, harsh reviews. Obedience was the trait Zipporah adored most in others.

This is where Riley comes in.

He was an eighteen-year-old patient who doubled as Zipporah's lapdog. They made for a surprisingly compatible duo. He was a rough skinhead from Stoke-on-Trent; she was a dreadlocked sadist who loved sycophants. He slobbered, she lengthened her leash.

Riley had a history of violence. He enjoyed 'dancing with Snow White', which muddled his head. He started mistaking his mother for the Royal Mint and tiefed from

her ass like she was bricking blocks of gold. When she
called the cops he grabbed a knife and sliced her salami-
pink face. The police busted him. But the devil danced in
his eyes. He pleaded insanity and landed here, where
Zipporah served as the perfect carer/drug-dealer, plying
him with all the Xanax, Ativan and Valium he could need.
Forget 'Snow White'. Boy was now big on Benzos.

Naturally, he had to earn his 'keep'. If an obstinate
patient refused to leave their room, Riley was sent to
harass them out. He once stole an old man's shoes. The
old man hobbled out on bare feet and complained to
Zipporah, who acted clueless. After wandering around the
ward for hours the old man started crying, and Riley
replaced the shoes where he had found them. Zipporah
recorded that the old man had left his room for three
hours that day and was improving. The old man slept in
his shoes that night.

The patients weren't the only ones being harassed.
When I came to work one day in high heels, Zippy was
not amused. No one else gave a shit. Zippy, however,
didn't think my love of bootleg Louboutins had any place
in her 'paradise' programme. So she set Riley on me.

I was preparing breakfast for the patients one morning when Riley snuck into the kitchen and grabbed my
ass. I turned and faced him. He flicked his tongue.

'Wanna fuck me?' he said.

I laughed. 'I don't fuck devil-spawn.'

He flinched. I stood still. He turned around and
bolted.

When I started serving breakfast Riley entered the
dining-hall, bubbling with spite. 'Fuck you, gaylord!' he
shouted.

I ignored him and handed out toast.

'Didn't you hear me, you *fucking* fag? You're the one
who belongs in here. Not us! You look like a crazy bitch!'

'You're downright disrespectful,' said the old man

whose shoes he had stolen.

'Let him have his moment,' I said. But his moment stretched to an hour, two hours, a day. At first he was all talk. But with each passing moment he took more liberties. I didn't file a complaint when he pressed his hands in between my thighs. In fact, I let him cop a feel. His tobacco-stained fingers ruffled up my skirt. But I let him enjoy. I let him caress me like we were badly drawn lovers in a weird, psychosexual edition of Mills & Boon. I didn't cringe when I caught his whiff. I didn't curl up and die when he started touching himself. I let him. And when he was done smacking his salami, I smirked (as you do). He enjoyed a free-for-all piss-take, which pissed me off. As he enjoyed my chicken cutlet boobs I began to calibrate my retaliation. Homeboy had to be put in check.

The idea hit me while I was on night-duty. Riley refused to take pills from 'a sket queer' and I figured it was time to correct him. After all the patients had gone to bed, I stole a syringe and filled it with water. I snuck into his room. It ponged of socks, semen and smoke. I shoved him awake. He stiffened at the feel of my syringe against his neck.

'Don't move,' I hissed. 'Don't make a sound. In fact, don't breathe.'

'What?'

'You're a determined little fucker, aintcha?'

'What do you want?' His voice was shaky.

'Poor baby,' I tutted. 'Don't you like the other side of harassment? You disturb my peace, I return the favour.'

'You won't get away with this.'

'This needle is filled with Pavulon. One little prick of this bad boy and your heart will stop in three minutes. You, my friend, will die a swift but agonising death.'

He was petrified. He began to hyperventilate. I leant closer.

'If you remain a bad little piggy, I'll be forced to kill

you. Comprende?'

He nodded.

'Good,' I said, putting a cap on the needle and shoving it into my pocket. As I was walking out, I turned around and said, 'I'd clean this room if I were you. It smells like death.'

The next morning, I was summoned to the Meeting Room. There was a circle in the centre, which consisted of chief-of-staff Dr. Feldman, Zipporah, Riley and his mother. Dr. Feldman tapped his notebook. Zipporah was poised, pen at the ready. Riley's mother was sweaty with rage. Riley quivered at the sight of me.

'What's the problem?' I said.

'You fucking tranny!' screamed Riley's mother. 'I can't believe you'd allow a tranny to be a nurse!'

'Mrs Granger, please,' said Dr. Feldman. 'This is a circle of trust.'

'The fuck are you on about?' she shouted. 'This bloody queen threatened to kill my son!'

'Excuse me?' I said.

'You heard me, Titty La Rouge! I'm not about to have my son sectioned for life because some homicidal transfanny tried to top him. It's a hospital for fuck's sake! And you're his nurse!'

'Look,' I turned to Dr. Feldman. 'When I signed up for this job, I knew there would be challenges. But it didn't include transphobic slurs and murder accusations.'

'Nurse Cat – ' began Dr. Feldman, nervously.

'Admit it!' burst out Zipporah.

'Admit what?'

'That you tried to kill this boy!'

'Yeah!' chimed the enraged mother. 'Admit it.'

'What did I threaten to kill him with?' I asked.

This stumped everyone for a second. They turned to Riley, who had bags under his eyes.

'Pav...Pav,' he stuttered.

'Yes?' encouraged Zipporah.

'Spit it out!' said the mother. 'I've got an appointment with Work Directions in an hour.'

'Puh...Pavilion,' said Riley. 'That's it! He tried to kill me with Pavilion!'

'What the fuck is 'Pavilion'?' asked the mother.

'Yes,' I said, 'what *is* 'Pavilion'?'

'It kills you,' said Riley.

'Are you sure it wasn't something else?' asked Zipporah.

'I'm sure,' said Riley.

I looked at Dr. Feldman, who was clearly clenching his butt-cheeks. I looked at Zipporah, whose jaw was tighter than a fist.

'Not to make this any more awkward for you,' I said, 'but not only will I take this incident to an employment tribunal, but I will sue the bejeezus out of this hospital for transphobia. You have repeatedly victimised me. Why, because I wear tights and a bit of slap? You compromised my physical and emotional safety by encouraging an environment of naked hostility towards me. To then accuse me of trying to murder a patient is despicable and unjust.'

I stormed out of the room. Twenty minutes later, they followed. Riley was weeping. Zipporah wasn't consoling him. Instead she looked shit-scared, like someone about to lose her job. The next day Riley was transferred to a different wing. A week later Zippy went on 'extended sick leave'.

Many months later I bumped into Riley outside the hospital. He had gained some weight and had a healthy glow in his cheeks. He was struggling to light his cigarette. He froze when he saw me. I didn't say anything. Instead I reached into my pocket and withdrew my own lighter. I lit it and held the fire towards him. He inched back. But when he saw that I wasn't trying to annihilate him, he moved closer. Close enough for me to smell him. He smelt of Nivea and coffee. He lit his cigarette. I shoved the lighter back into my pocket and started walking off.

'Thanks,' he called out. I smiled.

'Mon plaisir.'

NDAMBI

y sister tells me I'm living in sin. 'Tis true. But she doesn't conk that this is *my* sin. She tells me it is haram for a woman to love another woman. 'Tis also true. But I don't need to hear it from her.

She calls me on a regular to scope the situation, to sniff traces of melancholy and dissatisfaction in my voice. But I'm a psychoanalyst and this is pop psychology 101. I see it played out like a Carry On film on my ward every day. It's a game for rookies.

'How're you?' she asks.

'I'm fine, hon,' I say in a warm voice. 'Na wewe?'

'Alhamdulilah,' she says, although her timbre is slightly shaky, desperate to conceal. 'What you been up to?'

'Working,' I say. 'Things are hectic but exciting.'

'Hmm.' This is not what she wants to hear. 'And what about – ?' She pauses, expecting me to finish her sentence. I let the silence drag until I can hear her shallow breathing through the receiver.

'Adrienne?' I finally say with a smile. 'She's great. So sweet and gentle and' – I sigh for a blissed-out effect – '*giving*. She makes me feel like I'm the centre of the earth, like nothing else matters. Alhamdulilah!'

The silence becomes sound. With just a few carefully chosen words I've made incisions into her vital organs. Brick by brick her interior structure starts to crumble. That's when the sermon begins.

'Walaahi, I pray that you see the light,' she says with

the faux-sympathy of the faux-pious. 'I pray that the shatan leaves your spirit; I pray that you find a man because lesbianialism can be cured. I *pray* that Allah cures you. I *pray*. All you need to do is to find a good man and settle down.'

'Like you, right?'

My sister never finished high school because she wanted to play house with an illiterate bundu-boy from Bosaaso who subsequently made her drop five babies before she was thirty, then dumped her ass for an Egyptian teenager with an air-tight clit and cash to stash. But I don't state this. It's not my style.

'Abdi was a good father!' she fumes. 'He loved his kids!'

'Yes,' I say in a mellow voice. '*Loved*.'

My sister weighs my spite before she spits, 'Are you even human?'

'No,' I say. 'It's probably my *lesbianialism*. I think it's fucking up the rotation.'

'Maybe you need to check into a mental hospital.'

'Darling!' I gasp. 'Why you hurt me so! You know those places freak me out!'

'Hmmff! You shall chew lock one of these days.'

'Sister girl, I *always* chew lock, especially when you bell me. But you know how we do. We *maintain*.'

'No, sis,' she says, '*you* maintain while the rest of us carry bare burden.'

'Hawa,' I say, 'what do you want me to do for you?'

'I want – ' she sighs. 'I want you to say it'll be fine.'

'It'll be fine,' I say sincerely.

'How do you know?'

'I just do.'

She sighs a little more easily.

'How are the kids?' I ask.

'Alhamdulilah.'

'Tell them habo Ndambi will be over soon.'

'Ati Ndambi?' she sneers. 'Samira, when are you going to get real? Nobody calls themselves 'Ndambi'. Why'd you want to go from Samira to 'Sin'?'

'It's 'Ndambi,' not 'dhambi'. It means 'most beautiful'.'

'Oh please!' she says.

'Bye, Hawa,' I smile and hang up. After I put down the receiver I recline in my chair. I can hear one of my patients playing *Young Hearts Run Free* in their room. I prick up my ears, let the rhythm ride my pulse. Candi Staton was on point when she said self-preservation is what's really going on today.

Night-time

When I come home that evening I listen to my answering machine. There are no messages from Adrienne. I chuckle sadly to myself. Night-time is always the hardest. It's when the ghouls of my imagination play games with my sanity. So I get practical and run a bath. I lace the steaming water with oils and salts until the tub is slick. Adrienne used to do this for me every night after I came home from work. She used to buy 'bath bombs' which were fruity soaps that dissolved effervescently in water. I would emerge from the bathroom smelling of mango and sexual hunger. We would kiss like love-starved youts. She would press me hard against the wall, lick my lips, tongue would meet tits, hips, clit. She would melt me down until I stunk of sex and satisfaction. And then we would lie in bed and talk of all the love we had gained and everything we had lost. Those conversations were our way of fortifying the chord that connected us. What was once our temple, the place where we created love, has become my prison, a space custom-built for turmoil. So what to do? Should I sink further into funk and act stone-face outside these walls? Should I continue to not mention my loss to anyone?

Or...

Should I come harder?

I decide these questions don't need answers tonight. Tonight is about TV and takeaway and bourbon on ice. It's about dabbing attar on my collarbone and cotton sheets. Tonight is a date with Maxwell and Coco de Mer.

I remove my bra and panties, enjoy the curve of my breasts, the groove of my nipples. I squeeze the tips, feel them tighten. I run my palm under my powder-soft arms, massage each muscle until I moan. My body has not been touched in moons and tonight I want to sweat. My mind plays games with my body, directing my fingertips to the nook of my navel. But I don't fully touch skin. Instead, I suck my stomach in and close my eyes. I focus on my breathing.

I inhale.

Hold.

Release.

I do this until I am loose.

It is time.

Love Egg

I walk over to my closet and remove the box. It is black and the gold-leaf card attached to it reads:

The Jade Love Egg practice originated in ancient China. Taoist Masters taught the secrets of the Jade Egg only to a very small number of women: the Empress and the concubines. It was believed that these practices gave them longevity, youthful energy and extraordinary skills as lovers.

I carry the box to my bed. I lay it down and reach for the Arabian oils on my bedside table. I rub the oils over myself. The scent is musk and morning glory. I sprawl on the bed and open my thighs wide while Maxwell's *Em-*

brya steams up the room. Maxwell's falsetto is cream on wax and as I coax one, two, three fingers inside my pussy my toes curl. As I go deeper within myself the music sounds richer and the musk smells sweeter. I push my hips back and forth to take in my fingers. When I'm wet I wipe my hands on a towel. I open the Coco de Mer box and remove the jade egg. It is smooth, the size of a duck egg. I put it in my mouth to moisten it. As Maxwell's bass-line becomes my heartbeat, I drop the egg onto my palm. I trace it around my nipples, torso and pubic bone, which glisten with oil and sweat. I tease myself like this until my throat is dry, until I'm panting.

I'm tight so I slowly twerk the egg inside me. It's painful at first but I open up as I gently push and turn the semi-precious stone. The room feels so hot I can barely breathe. I inhale and exhale at a deep, hypnotic pace. I imagine Adrienne's tongue on my clit and my body starts building up to climax until I can no longer control my breath, until all I can do is howl. When I come the love egg pops out of me and I simply lie there, legs shaking. After I shower and as I drift off to sleep Maxwell's *Embrya* comes to an end. The final track is a recording of an ultrasound. The last thing I hear that night is a baby's heart beating inside my head.

Freedom

The Prophet once said that dreams are a window into the unseen. I have been told many times by family, friends, colleagues and strangers that I, a black African Muslim lesbian, am not included in this vision; that my dreams are a reflection of my upbringing in a decadent, amoral Western society that has corrupted who I really am. But who am I, really? Am I allowed to speak for myself or must my desires form the battleground for causes I do not care about? My answer to that is simple: 'no one *allows* anyone anything.' By rejecting that notion you discover that only you can give yourself permission on how to lead your life, naysayers be damned. In the end something gives way. The earth doesn't move but something shifts. That shift is change and change is the layman's lingo for that elusive state that lovers, dreamers, prophets and politicians call 'freedom'.

Do I think I'm free? Well, let a sister break it down for ya. I often dream of home. It is a place that exists only in my imagination: it is my Eden, my Janna. Sometimes I associate it with my father, my mother, my grandmother, my sister, all of whom have rejected me, all of whom I still love. Sometimes home takes the shape of my ex, Adrienne. I like to think that the memory of her beautiful Afro, spiky attitude and sweetness is sacred, that I worship at her altar. Other times, I regard Somalia, my birthplace, as home, as the land where my soul will eventually be laid to rest. Many times home is Kenya or London. But none of these places or people truly *embody* home for me. Home is in my hair, my lips, my arms, my thighs, my feet and hands. I am my own home. And when I wake up crying in the morning, thinking of how lonely I am, I pinch my skin, tug at my hair, remind myself that I am alive. Remind myself to step outside and greet the morning. Remind myself that it's all about forward motion. It's all about change. It's all about that elusive state.

Freedom.

EARTHLING

fter being discharged from the Maudsley Mental Hospital, Zeytun went to her local internet café to spy on her sister Hamdi's Facebook profile. The café was located at the bottom of Peckham Rye. A bad paint-job meant that the walls looked like they had been plastered with puke. The Somali man at the counter was startled by her appearance. She was wearing a housecoat with holes in it and oversized loafers; and even though her face was that of a woman in her mid-twenties, her long, scraggly hair was white. She slapped fifty pence down on the counter.

'Thirty minutes,' she said in Somali.

'Inna lillah!' the man muttered to himself. Zeytun ignored him and removed a can of Shaani from the fridge.

'That'll be 50p.'

Zeytun grudgingly produced the change. She opened the can and guzzled the drink.

'Slow down,' the man said as he handed her the computer-code. 'You'll get brain-freeze.'

Zeytun snatched the paper from him. 'I already have brain-freeze.'

'Are you okay?' asked the man. 'You're safe here, you know? No-one will hurt you.'

But Zeytun had already moved across the crowded room to find a booth. She felt uneasy as soon as she sat down. A Nigerian woman beside her was talking on Skype: 'Yes my darling...*no, this smelly Somali lesbian is sitting next to me*...Yes, the sermon was fantastic...yes, it is a shame but *dykes are such nasty creatures.* Adetoun talked to the pastor afterwards...*Hell, that's where you're headed, you dirty bitch.* The pastor was wonderfully insightful and of course, *lesbians are nothing but cheap whores.'*

Zeytun wanted to punch the woman. She knew she was hallucinating, but that didn't make the experience any less hurtful or real.

She looked around to see if her girlfriend Mari had followed her. After Mari had picked her up from the hospital Zeytun had told her that she wanted to go for a walk. Mari had grudgingly okayed this, but Zeytun knew Mari would panic if she discovered that she had gone to an Internet café. Zeytun understood Mari's reasons for disconnecting their home broadband but she was still resentful. Zeytun loved being connected to the wider world, to feast on Facebook. She loved it even though the Internet had almost killed her. She remembered trawling through dangerous websites, sweating with fear and excitement at the idea of taking her own life. She had played Meshell Ndegeocello's *Comfort Woman*, the album that she and Mari often made love to, and planned her self-extinction. Ndegeocello's space-age soul hymn to the power of loving another woman had been their anthem, but now neither Zeytun nor Mari could listen to that album without remembering the desperation of that time.

Sick sick sick sick dyke –

The Nigerian woman finished her call and left. Zeytun heaved a sigh of relief and logged on to her Facebook page. Her inbox was filled with messages, mostly from well-wishing friends, none from her sister, Hamdi. Zeytun didn't bother reading the messages. All she wanted was to see what was happening with Hamdi. She went on Hamdi's page and saw her face for the first time in six months. They hadn't spoken since their fight.

It was summer and they were both cooling themselves

off with a glass of cold Vimto in Hamdi's council flat in Shepherd's Bush. There had been a mice infestation: because the building was falling apart they had crawled in through every crevice. Hamdi had had pest control in repeatedly but the mice always returned. So Zeytun took some time off from her photographic assignments and came down to Hamdi's armed with a king-size bottle of rat poison and a baseball-bat.

'We're going to merk these muthafuckers,' she said, making a screw-face, and of course they laughed about the ridiculousness of the situation. Hamdi was scared of killing the mice but Zeytun relished it. She opened Hamdi's storage cupboard, which had been unused for the two years that she had lived in that flat, and discovered a horde of mice, some heavily pregnant. Zeytun killed every single one she could target and soon most of the pregnant ones, which had been slower than the others, were dead.

'Zeytun, those were mothers,' Hamdi said sadly as her sister scraped the tiny mashed corpses up with the dustpan and tipped them into the bin.

'They were also pure wasakh. Did you want to keep them?'

'No.'

'Then I guess that's that.'

'Haki, only a lezzo could be so hardboiled!'

'Yes, but look at how desperate you are for this hardboiled lezzo's help!'

'Touché.'

At that time both Zeytun and Hamdi were embarking on new relationships, Zeytun with Mari and Hamdi with a traditional man from their clan called Libaan, and there was a genuine sense of shared joy between the two sisters. Hamdi had never met Mari and was quite surprised when Zeytun told her that she was half-Somali half-Japanese. Even though Hamdi was still getting used to the idea of having a lesbian sister, she was supportive. Her new boyfriend, however, took a dim view. Two women 'fornicating' was unnatural and repulsive, not to mention 'haram'.

At first Hamdi was angry that Libaan was reacting this way about her sister. But she was also desperate to get married. She was twenty-nine and, since she viewed herself through a traditional Somali lens, practically an old maid. Libaan gave Hamdi an ultimatum: she had to choose between him and Zeytun. By then Zeytun was hearing voices in her head and it was the beginning of another descent into painful psychosis for her. Hamdi made her choice: Libaan.

She took a distinctly puritanical stance when she told Zeytun her decision.

'It's haram, Zey. It's against our beliefs.'

'No! It's against *your* beliefs! Anyway, you're only saying that to justify choosing him over me! I didn't choose to be a lesbian. Life is hard enough as it is. If Mari had given *me* such an ultimatum, I'd have told her to fuck off!'

'Well, I'm not you and I never will be.'

Zeytun headed for the door. Determined to have the last word, she shouted, 'I love Mari because she makes me happy. You love Libaan because he validates you. I'm glad I'm not you. Have a nice life!'

Zeytun gazed at Hamdi's Facebook pictures. They all showed Hamdi smiling. Here she was with her friends at a party, wearing a turquoise hijab, gold tooth glinting. Here she was in the arms of Libaan, who had a cigarette in the corner of his mouth – a habit Hamdi hated. His look was territorial. Another picture was set in Hamdi's kitchen and she looked content bent over the stove cooking suqaar, presumably for Libaan. Ever since she was little Hamdi had wanted nothing more than to be a wife and mother whereas Zeytun had dreamt of becoming a photographer and being out in the world, capturing it all without restraint. Zeytun used to take countless pictures of Hamdi on her Nikon camera: Hamdi had been her muse. She hadn't picked up her camera since she stopped speaking to Hamdi and she didn't think she could now: her confidence was gone.

Each photograph on the computer portrayed Hamdi as a woman satisfied with her life. Zeytun scrutinised her sister's face for traces of melancholy, some mirroring of the loss she felt, but found none.

There were 197 photos of friends, relatives, the fiancé, colleagues, and acquaintances in Hamdi's profile. None of them included Zeytun. She logged out and left the café.

Fucking dyke bitch die bitch...

As she walked from Peckham Rye towards her house in Lordship Lane in East Dulwich, Zeytun kept her headphones clamped to her head and blasted music on her iPod. The voices were coming from everywhere. She could hear insults from old women in cars even though their windows were shut. She could make out murder threats, but who were they coming from? The pedestrians on the street? The starlings and crows wheeling above her head? The Dalmatians and Labradors in the park, whose barks were encoded taunts aimed solely at her? The loud breathing of joggers brushing past her became wilfully pornographic and disgusting. A black teenage boy chirpsing a shy, pretty girl was plotting her rape and subsequent dismemberment, and then Zeytun's.

What frightened Zeytun was that even with her music blotting out the sounds she could still read these people's lips. Their abuse had a psychotic intensity. They were insane. They didn't even know her: why would they attack her so randomly? For being a lesbian? Did she look that butch? Was there a mark upon her forehead that disclosed her sexuality? *Please stop,* she wanted to scream. But instead the voices multiplied into a hostile chorus. Suddenly the fact she was a lesbian was no longer the only issue. There were now new insults to deal with:

'An ugly beggar.'

'Hamdi was right about you. You are pure muck.'

'Ohmigod, she's going to pick up a cigarette butt from the ground and smoke it. Go on smoke it, tramp.

'She probably has venereal diseases. Yuck!'

'Ugh! She's pissed herself.' Horrified, Zeytun touched her crotch to see if this was true. It wasn't. *'Psych!'* laughed the voices. *'You're one dumb bitch!'*

Determined not to be defeated, Zeytun cranked up the volume on her iPod and walked faster. As she neared her house, her heart began to thud. She was nearly at the finishing line, which was also, somehow, the moment of most extreme danger, the last possible place the inevitable assault could come. She resisted the temptation to run because running might be a trigger as it was with certain wild animals. *I'm not afraid*, she repeated to herself, although she was. She knew she was being watched. She wasn't sure by whom, but she knew. There were spies everywhere. Even the squirrels in the trees were suspects. She laughed a little uneasily at the thought. When she reached her front steps she couldn't take the anxiety anymore so she ran up to the door, and fumbled frantically with the keys. When she finally got it open she hurried inside but closed it quietly behind her.

She was greeted by the comforting aromas of cinnamon and coriander. Afraid to switch off her iPod in case the voices returned, instead she pressed 'pause' and pricked up her ears. Though she could still hear the voices trying to get through the front door there were no abusive taunts coming from inside the house. She sighed with relief. Why didn't the voices follow her inside? It was unnerving not knowing when and where they would strike next.

She walked slowly down the hallway and into the kitchen. Steam hit her face, warm and damp. Mari's back was to her and she was swaying her hips gently to the sound of Maryam Mursal on the watermelon-shaped stereo. She was humming to the song as she sliced tomatoes. She danced in such an innocently sensuous way that Zeytun simply stood there and watched her. *She is the reason the voices can't attack me here*, thought Zeytun. The house was not the sanctuary, Mari was. Her shoulder-length braids had seashells in them and when she moved her head the shells clacked against each other. She was wearing an orange guntino, a traditional Somali wraparound dress that had to be created daily by the wearer. It was this improvisational essence, and the fact the dress symbolised Somaliness, which appealed to Mari. Her mother Kinsi was Somali and her father Natsume was Japanese. They had met in Kenya in the late seventies and divorced shortly after Mari was born, so she never knew her father. It was ironic that even though Zeytun was born in Somalia and fully Somali, Mari, who had never been to the country and was mixed-race, appreciated Somali culture more than she did. In fact Mari identified wholly with Somaliness and referred to herself as a Somali, denying her Japanese heritage altogether.

One time Zeytun bought her a beautiful silk Japanese print of cherry blossoms. Mari smiled graciously and hung the picture in the guest bedroom.

Now Zeytun crept up behind her and delicately caressed her braids. Mari did a double-take and squealed.

'You scared the shit out of me,' she said trying to regain her breath. 'I was about to shank you one-time.'

'I'm sorry, hon, didn't mean to startle you.'

'Is alright,' Mari said uneasily. 'If you had been an intruder, I'd have served your guts for supper. With a bottle of Chianti and some fava beans.'

'It's lucky we're out of fava beans.'

'Oh, I'd have made it work. I'd have stewed those guts

so deliciously you'd literally be licking your fingers. You know I can throw down in the kitchen.'

'And in the bedroom, on the dining-table, on the carpet. You're a regular freak-a-leak.'

'What can I say? I'm a black Belle de Jour. Reading that tat actually gives me prostitution envy. I resent my mother for teaching me that my vagina is not a commodity.'

They laughed at this and Zeytun realised it was the first time she had laughed in months. The sound came loose and free. It reminded her of why she fell in love with Mari. Mari was warm, gentle. She had the ability to turn even the most gruesome event into a comic riff. The only thing she never joked about was Zeytun's illness, although Zeytun would have preferred it if she did.

'Are you hungry, macaan? Dinner will be ready soon. Just help yourself to a mango.'

'I could murder a mango,' said Zeytun, reaching for the fruit basket on the counter. 'With chili and lemon.'

'Sort yourself out, sugar mama. Mangia, mangia.'

Zeytun grabbed a mango and lemon. She opened the utensils drawer to retrieve a knife but there were none inside. There were no forks either. All that was inside were some tablespoons.

'Where're all the knives?' she asked.

'Oh, don't worry I'll cut this for you,' said Mari, taking the fruit from Zeytun's hand.

'What happened to all our knives and forks?' asked Zeytun, even though she knew the answer. Mari looked away from her and said, 'We have to be careful.'

They stood in silence for a moment. Zeytun turned away and left the kitchen.

'Don't you want your fruit?' Mari called after her.

'I've lost my appetite.'

She went into the living-room and sat on the sofa. It was old, and creaked heavily as she sank into it. She closed her eyes. She remembered the knife incident: the frightened expression on Mari's face that night; the nausea and fear she felt as she lay on their bed, knife in hand, waiting to strike.

It was five weeks ago. Mari had arranged a weekend break from the hospital for Zeytun. She had just changed medication and was recovering gradually. The previous medication had caused her to develop Parkinsonism, leading to tremors and an unstable posture. At one point the muscles in her arms and legs had tightened and bent her into a painful, pretzel shape like a contortionist. She had had to take Procyclidine to combat the side-effects of the antipsychotic. Her doctors then put her on a 50mg Risperidone depot, which was injected into her buttocks every fortnight. The new medication calmed her down and reduced the voices significantly.

Noticing the difference the medication was making, Mari took a chance and brought her home for a relaxing weekend. They stayed in and watched *All About Eve*, an old favourite of Mari's, and *High Art*, a dark lesbian romance which Zeytun loved. They ate, laughed and made mad love. At the end of the weekend, though, the hallucinations returned. Zeytun heard Mari sharpening a knife in the kitchen and thought she was planning to kill her. Sweating heavily, she strode into the kitchen where Mari was slicing a leg of lamb, opened the utensils drawer and removed a bread-knife.

'Zeytun, what're you doing?' asked Mari, alarmed.

'You're not going to kill me!' Zeytun screamed and ran off to their bedroom. She locked the bedroom door and went and sat on the bed, ready to defend herself. She waited and waited for Mari to come into the bedroom but she never did. After a long night of waiting, Zeytun finally dozed off, the knife still in her hand.

In the morning, she was woken by a knock on the door.

'Zeytun, its Edo Kinsi. Open the door, hon.'

Could Mari's mother be trusted?

'I just want to talk to you, sweetheart.'

Zeytun wasn't convinced. She groped about for the knife where it had fallen to the floor. 'Stand back,' she called. Then she opened the door. Kinsi looked tired. Her eyes were red and her nappy Afro was not covered up in a hijab like it usually was. She was wearing a long denim skirt and a green cardigan. Between her eyebrows the faded tattoo of a Japanese character was puckered with concern.

'Edo, I thought you were doing well. Mari was so excited to have you home. What happened?'

'She's trying to kill me,' muttered Zeytun. 'Please don't let her kill me.'

'Zey, Mari loves you. She'd never hurt you. She's worried sick about you.' Kinsi's eyes went to the knife in Zeytun's hand. 'She didn't want to call the hospital because she was afraid they'd section you for longer. At the same time she didn't know if you were going to harm yourself. That girl is crazy about you.'

Zeytun sat on the bed and whispered, 'I'm afraid of losing her.'

'You won't lose her,' promised Kinsi. 'You just need to concentrate on getting better.'

It was Kinsi who drove her back to the Maudsley. Mari sat in the passenger seat, looking tired and staring out into the ash-grey sky. Zeytun sat in the back, listening to her iPod, trying to drown out the voices. She hallucinated that she was naked and tried to cover her vagina with her hands. Snap! Pop! Her clothes were back on but her face burned with shame.

When they reached the ward Kinsi waited in the reception area while Mari went in with Zeytun to speak to her consultant, Dr. Feldman. He questioned Mari about Zeytun.

'Did you guys have a good weekend?' he asked, scribbling on his notepad.

'Yes,' said Mari. Her voice was shaky. 'We had a great time.'

'Were they any changes to Zeytun's behaviour?'

'No, she was excellent.' Mari bit her lip, and for a moment Zeytun thought she was going to tell the doctor the truth. If so, Zeytun would be sectioned for the winter. She started sweating. Mari looked at her for the first time that day. Her eyes were moist, her lips dry. Zeytun realised that Mari's gaze betrayed something less noble than love: pity.

The dream tasted as sweet as halwa. Zeytun and Hamdi were young girls. Their mother Roda was driving them to Splash!, the water-park in Nairobi. They giggled loudly in the back of the car and played rock-paper-scissors. For some reason Zeytun always chose paper and Hamdi scissors. 'Not fair!' squealed Zeytun, tugging at her pigtails.

Hamdi's hair, which was long and silky, was tied back in a tight bun. 'Nya-nya-boo-boo, you've lost again!'

'Hooyo,' said Zeytun, 'Hamdi is not playing fair!'

'Girls, you better act right,' said Roda, looking in the rear-view mirror. 'Otherwise we're heading straight back home.' This made the games stop completely: they knew their mother meant what she said. Roda smiled to herself and steered the Peugeot down the pot-holed road towards Splash!

Once they were inside the amusement park they got out of the car and headed for the changing-room. Young girls and boys in swimsuits milled about with their mothers. Zeytun's swimsuit was brown and yellow with cheap plastic sunflowers stitched across the neckline. Hamdi, on the other hand, had insisted on a lavender Adidas one-piece that had cost their mother nearly half her monthly wages. Roda worked as a paediatric nurse in Kenyatta Hospital and money was tight. But she still managed to treat her daughters to Splash! or a meal at Steers every once in a while.

There were two large slides in the park, an open white one and a closed red one.

'Let's go on the red one,' said Hamdi as they joined the queue.

'Hayaye! I'm scared,' said Zeytun. It was Hamdi who had been the fearless one as a child: as they got older Zeytun became bolder.

'We'll do it together,' said Hamdi, holding her hand. 'Walaahi, I'll protect you.'

Zeytun reluctantly acquiesced. So they held onto each other at the top of the slide. 'Don't let go,' said Zeytun. 'I promise not to,' said Hamdi, kissing her.

Off they went, squealing, zigging and zagging down the slide before plunging into a small pool at the other end. Roda, camera at the ready, snapped away like crazy as the girls hugged and posed for pictures. As they did this, Zeytun whispered to Hamdi, 'I really need to pee.'

'Me too,' giggled Hamdi. 'Let's just do it in the pool.'

'Ew,' said Zeytun, 'That's niggedy-nasty.'

'I'll do it if you will,' said Hamdi, eyes glinting.

Roda was still obliviously taking pictures of them. They tried to look inconspicuous. Slowly, a small yellow circle formed around them in the pool. Roda stopped taking pictures and stared at them in disbelief.

'Nacalad baa nigutaalo! Get the hell out of there, you dirty little brats. Akhas! How could you do that? Wait until I catch you and strangle you.'

But by then the girls had leapt out the pool and were running back up the stairs to the slides, to do it all over again.

'Zeytun! Zeytun!' her mother called. But it wasn't her mother's voice.

'Zeytun, wake up!' It was Mari, shaking her. Zeytun opened her eyes and felt dampness between her thighs. She realised she had wet herself.

'Don't worry about it,' said Mari with forced brightness as Zeytun quickly got out of bed. 'It's probably the medication. Hop in the shower. I'll change the sheets.'

Zeytun removed her bra and sodden Bugs Bunny boxers and went into the bathroom. As she turned on the shower she couldn't help smiling at the deliciousness of the dream.

Zeytun woke to the sound of something scratching at her bedroom window. She pulled the curtains and saw the words 'DYKE CUNT' trying to break the glass. It was like a macabre cartoon. *I'm not afraid*, she had to remind herself, although that didn't reassure her much. She tip-toed downstairs to the kitchen and noticed a note attached to the fridge. It read:

Hey lover,

Just popped to the café for a few hours. There's buttered pancakes on the counter as well as your Risperidone tablet. Please eat and take your meds. Will be back by lunchtime. Call me if you need anything.

Love you.

Mx

Zeytun made some ginger tea and took the plate of pancakes out to the patio. Before she began to eat she rolled a cigarette, which she puffed on between mouthfuls of pancake. There was nothing more satisfying than smoking and eating at the same time.

It had been the end of the summer, she had just moved in with Mari, she wasn't speaking to Hamdi, and the psychosis was paralysing her. She couldn't sleep or eat. She would often get up in the middle of the night, sit out on the patio and smoke until sunrise. She started dreaming of death. It seemed like a relief. She went on a website that listed every possible method for killing oneself. Some methods were conventional (such as sleeping pills with alcohol), while others were bizarre (such as drinking gallons of water until all the salt in your system was washed out). It was through this site that Zeytun first learned about death by tobacco. For some reason she found the idea funny. Also it involved just a few household ingredients. She wrote down the recipe and went to work. She had to do it at a time when Mari was at the café. She bought 25g of Old Holborn tobacco and boiled some water. She then poured the tobacco and hot water into a cup and left it to ferment for a day, then strained the results. The following evening, while Mari was out working, Zeytun put on clean underwear and played Meshell Ndegeocello's *Comfort Woman*. There were no tears, just a sense of finality. By now, the tobacco had become pure poison and it looked like treacle. Its taste was spectacularly bitter. She chased it down with a shot of brandy and went to bed.

The next thing she saw were bright lights and she thought, *I'm in heaven*. In fact she was at the A&E in King's College Hospital, about to have her stomach pumped. Mari cried and Zeytun felt sorry for her. As soon as her stomach was pumped she was sectioned at the Maudsley Mental Hospital.

She didn't like to think of that period and neither did Mari. Still smoking, she carried her plate back into the house and took her medication. She could feel the voices getting less noisy and she knew that if she took her tablets consistently for a few more weeks they might disappear completely. She couldn't wait. The voices interfered with her thoughts, made her barely able to function. Some days she felt like she had no personality. But Mari reassured her it was the trauma of the illness that made her feel this way, and not some genuine interior lack.

She went upstairs to their bedroom and pulled her suitcase of photographs from under the bed. As she unzipped it the first picture her eyes landed on was the one taken when she was a child peeing in the Splash! pool with Hamdi. Their expressions were conspiratorial as they looked cheekily at the camera. The next picture had been taken on Hamdi's eighteenth birthday and she was wearing a red hijab with gardenias. Zeytun's hair was black back then, and as Hamdi blew out her candles Zeytun had planted a kiss on her cheek. She felt a tug at her chest as she looked at these photographs. There were many of Hamdi posing for Zeytun. Hamdi didn't enjoy being photographed but she trusted Zeytun enough to let her photograph her repeatedly. There were photos of them with their mother Roda, smiling and looking satisfied. Then came the series of painful portraits that Zeytun had done when Roda was undergoing chemotherapy for cervical cancer. The black and white pictures showed their mother with her hair falling out, looking gaunt and slightly bemused by all the fuss. She had raised them by herself after their father, Omar, a journalist for the BBC, had been kidnapped and then killed in Somalia. Roda had died in Kenya, two years before Zeytun and Hamdi were sponsored by an uncle to move to London. Whilst Hamdi coped well, Zeytun disintegrated and lost her grip on reality. That was the beginning of her psychosis.

She stuffed the photos back into the suitcase and zipped it up. She then grabbed her camera and her iPod and left the house.

Nunhead Cemetery was one of the most beautiful and gothic cemeteries in London. At night it was eerie, but during the day mothers would push their prams along the gravelled paths and joggers would run about as if it was any public park. Some days there were even funfairs on the grounds. Children would eat ice cream whilst their parents lolled about a few metres away from the graves. There would be second-hand book sales and car-boot sales. The descendants of the dead would pay tribute to their loved ones while taking their dogs out for a walk.

Zeytun loved this cemetery. Even though she was a Muslim she often came here to mourn for her mother. There were crosses everywhere but she didn't care: she felt at peace with herself in this place. She took her camera and snapped pictures of the gravestones, of old dog bones, of joggers and lovers. Having a camera in her hand again was like holding the body of a lover. She snapped away and, in her concentration, found brief respite from her psychosis.

After visiting the cemetery Zeytun snuck off to the internet café on Peckham Rye again. She bought a can of Shaani and sat in the farthest corner of the café, playing Cassandra Wilson's *Thunderbird* loudly on her iPod. *With the music so loud*, she thought, *at least these people won't invade my thoughts*. She felt tense and rigid as she logged on to her Facebook page. Her heart started pumping. What if there was a message from Hamdi? She could only hope.

There were no emails from Hamdi but there was a strange status update. It read:

'*Walapa walapa.*
So the wedding is two Saturdays from now and it'll be at Woolwich Town Hall. For those of you who haven't received an invite, consider this your invite.

Love,
Hamdi'

Zeytun felt like she had been punched. It had been a given that she would be a bridesmaid at her sister's wedding but now she had to find out about it through Facebook? She wanted to smash the computer screen.

Instead, she got up and fled the café as a chorus of voices screamed, 'You're the silliest, dirtiest puttana. Fucking die!'

It was after they had made love that night that Zeytun decided to tell Mari about Hamdi's wedding. Mari sighed and spooned Zeytun, wrapping her arms around her breasts. 'I think you should go,' said Mari. 'Hamdi might have acted shadily but she's your sister and you two have been through a lot together.'

'She won't answer the phone to me.'

'Go to the wedding. Talk to her then.'

'It could get really awkward.'

'I think she's as miserable without you as you are without her. Scope the situation. I'll drive you down there and wait in the car while you talk to her.'

'I'm really nervous, hon.'

'It'll give you peace of mind to know that you've tried. Give it a shot. In fact, come down to the café tomorrow and paint a plate for her.'

'You think?'

'I'm sure she'll appreciate it.'

'You're such a sweetheart,' said Zeytun, twisting around and kissing her on the lips.

Mari's café was a combined ceramics café and art studio on the corner of Lordship Lane and it was called Earthling. Mari usually made the ceramics herself and they ranged from small piggy-banks to ornate pots and calabashes to mugs shaped like cartoon monsters. She made the ceramics and the mostly well-to-do customers paid to paint them. After they had finished she would glaze the pieces and fire them. Sometimes mothers came in and had their babies' fingerprints imprinted on plates as keepsakes. Whilst the customers unleashed their inner artists Mari would serve them an assortment of teas, home-baked fudge cakes and key lime pie.

It was during a random visit to Earthling that Zeytun had first met Mari. They had hit it off immediately and after two weeks of intense conversations had had equally intense sex. One night Zeytun asked Mari, 'Why did you call your café Earthling?'

"Earthling' was actually obscure Victorian slang for lesbian.'

'So I can stop referring to myself as a lesbian now and say I'm an earthling.'

'It certainly gives it a dope flavour.'

'Bella.'

'Extra bella.'

Zeytun arrived just as a table of four women were leaving. At a neighbouring table Kinsi was doing the accounts. It was Mari who came up with the concept for the café and Kinsi who had bankrolled it.

'Zey,' smiled Kinsi, getting up and giving her a kiss on the cheek. 'You look really well.'

'I feel better, Edo,' said Zeytun. 'I'm not hearing too many voices now, although I still have to keep my iPod on standby.'

'Can I tempt you with a cuppa?' Kinsi asked. 'I'm not talking about the muck Mari serves in this place but some ginger shaax.'

'My body is calling for some shaax. Grazie Edo.'

Whilst Kinsi was making the tea Mari emerged from the studio. Below a clear, plastic apron she was wearing a transparent yellow dirac with a white petticoat. She removed her apron and kissed Zeytun on the lips.

'Are you ready to get your paint on?'

'I was thinking of that beautiful calabash,' said Zeytun, pointing to it on the shelf.

'You have a good eye, madamoiselle. That's my pièce de résistance,' said Mari, handing her the calabash.

'How much do I owe you for it, baby?'

'A lifetime of uninterrupted sex.'

'You girls are so nasty,' said Kinsi walking over with a pot of tea and three mugs. 'Is that all lesbians do? Talk of sex?'

'You're right Hooyo,' smiled Mari, 'we do apologise. And yes, all lesbians do is talk about sex.'

Even Kinsi couldn't help smiling at that. 'Nasty-nasty.' She set the pot and mugs down and pulled up a chair. Zeytun told her about Hamdi's impending wedding and her plan to attend it.

'I think she should have told you about the wedding,' said Kinsi, 'but I also think she's very scared of being rejected by you. She acted foolishly. But I know your sister is praying that you will attend the wedding.'

'But what will I say to her? I'm dreading seeing her.'

'I think you should feel sorry for her, because while you're moving on with your life with a partner who loves you completely, she's getting into a marriage where she has to leave half of herself at the door. That's no way to live. She's got that to learn.'

'Also,' chimed in Mari, handing paints to Zeytun, 'she must be miserable planning this wedding alone.'

Zeytun thought about this. She dipped a brush in the paint and started working on the calabash, determined that it should be a thing of beauty, in colours so harmonious they would heal any rift.

It was the night of the wedding, and Zeytun and Mari were driving down to Woolwich Town Hall. Mari had straightened Zeytun's white hair and braided it into a long plait. 'You look as regal as Toni Morrison,' she said, kissing her lips.

'I don't feel as wise though.'

'Even Toni has it tough sometimes.'

'Hmm.'

Zeytun wore a charcoal-grey trouser-suit. She had

sprayed herself with Sure deodorant. Mari had insisted that she at least dab some Dior perfume on her neck for the occasion. Zeytun had relented. So here they were, driving to the venue. Zeytun felt she might throw up. Mari on the other hand kept her composure. She was dressed appropriately for the occasion even though she wasn't going to go in. She wore a shimmering turquoise dirac with gold stitching that made her look like a mermaid, and around her neck a gold Nefertiti necklace that Zeytun had given her for her twenty-fifth birthday. The necklace had originally belonged to Zeytun's mother, Roda. Mari had been so touched by the gift that she cried.

Zeytun shifted anxiously in her seat as they approached Woolwich. 'She's going to spit in your face,' snarled the voices, 'she's going to make a fool of you.' Zeytun was tempted to tell Mari to turn the car around and drive back home. What was she doing? She didn't want to do this. What if the guests attacked her for being a lesbian? What if they all knew? She could hear them sneering, 'Khaniisad.'

I am a khaniisad, she thought, *I'm a lesbian and I'm fucking proud of it. So what? What's the worst that can happen?*

They drew up across the street from the town hall. Somali men and women in colourful outfits were milling outside, talking on mobile phones, the women applying lipstick, the men smoking. Zeytun recognised a few distant kinsfolk.

'I can't do this,' she said.

'You'll be fine,' said Mari, kissing her. 'Don't be afraid.' She handed Zeytun her purse and the calabash, which was wrapped in purple paper. Zeytun got out of the car and headed inside the hall holding her gift protectively in front of her, her purse jammed up awkwardly under one arm.

The wedding was in full swing. A Somali jazz band

was playing loudly although the acoustics were poor. Young girls in hijabs and boys in suits were running around while Indian waiters served the food. On the ceiling were a few balloons, and a pink banner had been hung across the end wall that read *Congratulations Libaan and Hamdi!* Despite the frenetic playing of the band the dance-floor was empty and the men and women weren't interacting with each other. The newlyweds were seated on plastic gold thrones on a platform at the far end of the hall. Hamdi wore a white hijab with gardenias and a silky Victorian-style dress whilst Libaan wore a white tux and white shoes. Even though it was their wedding and they were there to be admired, they didn't look like they were enjoying themselves. Hamdi looked tearful and Zeytun wanted to embrace her. As she moved towards the stage, one of the Indian waiters bumped into her and she dropped her calabash. It smashed onto the floor and everyone, including Hamdi, turned to look at her.

'Zeytun?' said Hamdi, but by then Zeytun had already turned and was running out of the hall. On her way out she collided with an aunt that she disliked. The aunt, who was a gossipy old woman, said, 'Zeytun, dear, how're you? Where have you been lately?'

'Oh fuck off, Edo!' said Zeytun, running out into the car-park. The aunt shouted curses at her as she looked around frantically for Mari. Her heart was in her mouth, beating on her tongue. 'You should never have come,' said the voices. 'It was a big mistake. You're a big mistake.' She had even brought her camera with her, like a fool. She saw the car.

'Zeytun, wait!'

She turned around and there Hamdi was, on her own in the entrance of the hall. They stood in silence for a few moments, watching each other. The aunt that Zeytun had insulted came outside to drag Hamdi back to the wedding.

'Leave her,' said the old woman, sneering. 'She's an ungrateful khaniisad.'

'Oh fuck off, Edo!' Hamdi snapped. Zeytun laughed. Hamdi came down the stairs leaving the old woman melodramatically fluttering her hand over her breast. Hamdi was now standing before Zeytun.

'You didn't invite me,' said Zeytun, finally.

'I was afraid you wouldn't come.'

'So you decided not to invite me anyway.'

'Zey, I'm sorry if I hurt you – '

'Yes, you did hurt me.'

'I just wanted the wedding to be a success.'

'Sorry I spoiled it for you then,' Zeytun snapped.

'I didn't mean it like that – '

'Didn't you?'

'Come back inside, Zeytun.'

Zeytun brushed a tear from her eye. 'No, I can't do that.'

'Why not?'

'You don't really want me here.'

Behind Hamdi, Libaan appeared in the doorway.

'Hamdi, come back inside,' he called.

'In a minute!' said Hamdi impatiently. She and Zeytun stood facing each other, groping for words. Then Zeytun turned, walked back to the car and got in. Without missing a beat, Mari started the engine and they drove off.

'She's gone,' Zeytun cried quietly. Mari patted her on her back with one hand, steering the car with the other. By the time they reached Blackheath Zeytun had calmed down. She selected an album on her iPod and plugged it into the car system. It was Meshell Ndegeocello's *Comfort Woman*. They both listened in silence. The sweetness of each song made the long journey bearable. They drove through Deptford and New Cross, with their deteriorated buildings and derelicts, and although Zeytun hated these neighbourhoods something was different tonight. The streetlights glowed brighter and the tramps looked less menacing. Had this place and its people changed? What made South London look beautiful tonight? Was it the sudden lack of noise in her head, the sense of clarity? The sound of her own voice saying, I'm almost there?

I'm almost free.

YOUR SILENCE WILL NOT PROTECT YOU

t required strength to make the call. I prayed on it. Not the usual prayer that my parents had taught me, that I had been caned and cajoled into practising when I was younger: this was more primal and urgent. As the voices grew louder I began to tremble. I hadn't slept or eaten properly for weeks.

It was a simple prayer. 'Allah, you have brought me here. Please help me.' I closed my eyes and in the pitch-black babble of voices and hysteria I found myself getting up from the settee and picking up my mobile phone. I entered the number without thinking about it.

'999. What's your emergency?' asked the female operator.

'I'm having a psychotic episode,' I replied in a shaky voice.

'How long have you been feeling this way?'

'Two months. No, two weeks. Two days. I think.'

'Okay.' She sounded sceptical. 'What are your symptoms?'

'I'm hearing voices, I'm anxious and I'm sweating. I need help.' I choked on the last word.

'Do you have any knives or sharp objects lying around?'

'I'm not going to kill myself. I just need help.'

'What's your address?'

I gave it to her.

'The ambulance is on its way. Remain calm and they will be with you shortly. If you think you'll have trouble answering the door, please leave it unlocked.'

She hung up. I sat there in the dark, foetid room and looked around. It was an open-plan flat so the kitchen and living-room were combined. The dustbin was over-flowing with rubbish, the sink smelt like sewage and I hadn't washed or brushed my teeth in weeks. I blamed the flat. There was nothing wrong with it, but I associated it with isolation, silence and inertia. I sank into self-pity: nothing could relieve the agonising chorus of voices in my head. If this was a mental problem why did it feel so physically painful? Why did it feel like my skull was being scraped out?

When the psychiatrist at the A&E asked me how I felt, I told her that I felt like my skull had been scraped out.

'You're very articulate,' she said, as if this was a fail-ing. 'What can I do for you?'

'Give me a sleeping pill.'

'I'll give you Lorazepam. Your father and brother are on their way from London. Stay put.' She brought me the pill and a glass of water, and left.

The tranquiliser started working instantly, and before I knew it I was in a strange, reassuring space where part of my brain had gone to sleep and the other part was diluting the voices until they were faint crackles: a transistor radio still picking up signals but at a low volume. I walked around the hospital with my eyes open but with every other sense dulled. I blinked and an hour later found myself being woken up by an orderly. I had fallen asleep on a bench outside the hospital. The orderly took my hand and led me back inside. 'Your father and brother are here for you,' he said.

I was too sluggish to even speak, but through my haze I could sense my father's irritation. I was the fourth child in a family of twelve, and even though I was creative and ambitious, even though I was studying on a prestigious course and trying to create a life for myself, my father had always harboured bigger dreams for me, dreams that I had always fallen short of fulfilling. Out of all my siblings he had invested the most time, money and energy in me.

When we were living in Nairobi I was the one who was sent to the expensive private school, whilst my more academically-gifted siblings were denied that privilege. During my teenage years, while my brothers and sisters were working hard at their studies, I was out getting drunk and smoking inordinate amounts of weed, stumbling home and vomiting on my bed. My father didn't care what I did – whether I chose to become a fashion-designer or a painter or a writer – he just wanted me to succeed, and the fact that I didn't frustrated him greatly. In a sense he viewed my mental illness as yet another failure on my part. He didn't see my psychosis as illness, but as an inability to square up to reality and become a responsible adult. To him even psychosis could be remedied with plenty of exercise, a healthy diet and unceasing activity. His pragmatism was an attempt to gain power over something that was simply beyond his control.

After we left the hospital we rode silently in a cab to the coach station and took separate seats on the coach. By the time we reached London the medication was wearing off and the aural and visual hallucinations had returned. I kept quiet about them. My father and my older brother took me to the family home but I didn't want anyone to see my shame. I didn't want my mum or younger siblings to see me looking so haggard and visibly ill. My aunt placed a plate of spaghetti on the kitchen table in front of me.

'Eat,' encouraged my dad. 'You need to keep up your strength.' But my family home turned a muddy shade of brown and my entire family morphed into soul-sucking leeches before my eyes. Even my niece, who was an adorable toddler, became a source of obscure resentment.

The line between my conscious thoughts and the part of my subconscious that harboured unlimited secret fears was being kicked over by false perception. Silence became my self-protection. Even though I was hungry I left the plate of pasta untouched and walked out of the house.

I holed up in my flat in Peckham, threw my mobile phone away and stopped speaking to anyone. I gave strict orders to my family to stop calling or visiting me as I wanted to recover without feeling any guilt and shame over my condition as I did so. In Somali culture mental illness is a taboo subject and I wanted to hide, which I did.

My only visitors were the nurses that arrived with my medication, and I rarely exchanged more than five sentences with them. I went from being a gregarious, apparently happy young man to a recluse who didn't speak to anyone and was suspicious of everything. I vegetated on the couch and gorged on ice-cream, curry, pizza, cake. I overate in the delusional belief that if I didn't gorge I would starve.

My saving grace came in the form of my older sister. She lived in a suburb in North London, over an hour's drive away, but still she came. I refused to let her in at first – I didn't want her to see my flat looking so filthy – but she gently convinced me to let her enter. Her husband had driven her and was waiting outside the block with my little niece and nephew. My sister discreetly told him to take the children to the park. Then, without missing a beat, she started cleaning up my house. I tried to stop her but she didn't want to hear it. Embarrassed, I went out onto the balcony and sat there, praying she would leave soon. But she didn't. Without judgement and with military efficiency she cleaned the bathroom, toilet, kitchen, living-room and bedroom and she was done in under an hour. During that time she talked to me. Not as an invalid but as her brother. I realised through her eyes that I hadn't changed at all: I was still the same person but I was just going through a tough time. One of my sister's most endearing qualities was that she always cracked jokes to make light of a bad situation. She told me hilarious stories about the ins and outs of the family, filling me in on all the soap-opera dramatics I had missed. She wasn't constrained around me. That day I felt human again. By the time her husband returned with the kids the house was sparkling and my sister had made lunch. She fed us all and when she was done she and the family left. The minute they walked out of the door I burst into tears of gratitude.

A few weeks later her husband went on a work trip and my sister invited me to stay over at her house and keep her company. I knew she wanted to keep *me* company but was being gracious about it. It was summer and our younger sister joined us as well. We watched light-hearted films and talked and laughed. When I was around them I forgot about my sadness and fear and anxiety. When I was around them I couldn't stop talking or telling jokes.

With my older sister's encouragement I applied for an internship at a small arts magazine called *Live Listings* and graduated from there to *Touch*, a hip-hop publication, and eventually to *Time Out London*. With each progression I became a little bolder. Something within me had shifted. I was unafraid to take on challenges that had seemed overwhelming before. Although I was still slightly awkward with people I relished my work and did it well. Within six months I was ready to go back to university and finish my degree.

I didn't want to go back to living in Birmingham but I had to attend classes there. What to do? My sister and I devised a simple but extreme solution: I would commute to Birmingham for each class and leave immediately afterwards. She would help pay the coach fare. It meant waking up at 3.30 a.m. every morning and leaving the house at 4.30 in order to catch the 6am coach from Victoria Coach Station. The classes started at 9 a.m.

It was a punishing routine, but I reckoned that I could spend the morning commute catching up on sleep and the return journey working on my assignments. I wrote my entire dissertation on the National Express coach and obtained a first. My father had never looked as proud of me as he did on my graduation day.

But that celebratory spirit would soon come to an end.

In the summer of 2006, after an argument with my father that was superficially about why I was not being more proactive in my life but was really, as far as I was concerned, about something else, I took the Number 149 bus from London Bridge and went to my sister's house in North London. She could see I was distressed and asked me what had happened. I became emotional and found myself choking on my words.

'Abaayo, I have something to tell you,' I said anxiously. I think she knew what was coming next and her expression grew slightly panicked. But she bit her lip and told me to carry on. I told her that I was gay.

She looked frightened by this revelation, but it seemed only because I had just uttered the unspeakable, because she gathered herself and reassured me that it would be fine.

We spent the rest of the afternoon and early evening in a state of heightened awkwardness. But as we went out to get milk for her kids from the local Turkish supermarket she said, 'I will support you. You're my brother and I'll support you.' Then she laughed. 'It's funny because this explains so much! And I feel weirdly closer to you as a result.'

Relieved that I had shared this secret with her, I went home and slept peacefully for the first time in years.

After I graduated from Birmingham I found myself without a job and my sense of isolation returned. I'm a social creature and I found living on my own a challenging experience, as I associated living on one's own with the beginning of a descent into another psychotic episode. Though it was a one-bedroom flat, my older sister suggested that I have my younger sister live with me. She could have my room and I was happy to sleep on the sofa in the living-room. I welcomed the idea of having company in the house and my younger sister had a delicious vibrancy about her. We would watch reruns of *Sex and the City* together and remark upon how daft Carrie Bradshaw was whilst secretly admiring the dramatics of her romantic entanglements. We would go to the cinema together and come home and share playlists with each other. We would dissect her relationships and I would often joke that she was the other half of my brain.

My younger sister's move into my home brought me a great deal of peace and calm. It was at this point that I met JT. He was a novelist, playwright, artist and screenwriter. We had begun corresponding on Gaydar, the popular dating site, and we instantly hit it off. We would write long emails to each other every day and when we finally met in Balans Café in Soho, we couldn't keep our hands off each other. I had never been in a serious long-term relationship before, mainly out of fear of being outed, but here was a man who made me feel wanted and needed and the feeling was mutual.

Love has a strange way of clarifying things, bringing order to chaos and making one feel bolder and more self-assured. JT did that for me.

At night we would talk about our lives, about where we had been in the past and who we had loved. A few weeks into our relationship I told him I suffered from schizophrenia, and without missing a beat he kissed me and reassured me that I had his full support. The next morning I left his place feeling so optimistic that I did a little skip on my way to the station.

When I came out to my younger sister she took it in her stride. 'I always knew!' she joked. 'I always knew!'

So things were on a genuine upswing. Then, as my relationship with JT grew more serious, my older sister started to worry. She was fine with me being gay when I was celibate but I would spend hours on the phone with JT whenever I was at her house, and her initial solidarity started to wane. One day, she sat me down and said, 'What you're doing is against our culture. It's against our faith. You have to stop.'

I was taken aback and I told her so. 'I thought you didn't mind me being gay?'

'I mind because it's against our beliefs.'

What I correctly read into that was that my older sister was embarrassed and, despite her earlier promises of support, didn't want to associate herself with the shame of having a proudly gay brother. The Somali community is all about tradition and that sense of tradition comes with an air of secretiveness, suppression and Puritanism. I had no desire to live in secrecy anymore. I had experienced what it was like to lead an open, healthy, guilt-free life and I liked it. It felt natural and necessary. I wasn't ready to come out to my entire family yet but as it turned out I had no say in the matter: my sister sped up the process for me.

I got a text from my older brother one evening, saying that he was coming to my house over the weekend. I texted him back, asking why. He simply replied that I should prepare myself. I immediately called my sister and asked her whether she told him about my sexuality. She replied yes.

'You're not going to listen to me because I'm a woman. You're not afraid of me but they'll talk some sense into you.'

I called her a vindictive bitch and hung up. I then texted my brother back and said, 'I know why you're coming to my house on Saturday but I don't want you there.'

He responded, 'I'll teach you a lesson and you'll stop these games.'

As humans we differentiate ourselves from all other species by claiming that empathy and 'human feeling' make us superior beings. But empathy is not a universal human trait. It cannot be learnt in books or taught in schools. A scholar in Classics may not possess the same level of empathy that an uneducated derelict may have.

It was whilst looking at my brother's text and contemplating what to do that I received a call from my eldest brother.

I had never liked my eldest brother. He was cocky in a charmless way. I picked up the phone.

The first words he said to me were, 'You're gay. Yuck!'

My response was 'I'm gay and I'm happy being gay.'

There was a moment's silence. 'You're no brother of mine. My brother can't be a fag.'

'Nobody is asking you to stick around. If you don't want me as your brother, I won't cry about it.'

He couldn't believe my nerve, so he tried another tactic. 'I know a lot of guys in London who would happily kill you.'

That's when I hung up the phone.

Regardless of how it's dressed up, whether it's presented as love from family or friends, abuse is abuse and I was unwilling to put up with it.

I washed my face, brushed my teeth, gelled my hair and put on carefully-ironed clothes. I called up JT at his workplace and told him what had happened. He urged me to go to the police-station, not realising that I was already on my way there.

After being kept waiting for hours at Peckham Police Station I was tempted to give up, go back home, curl up in bed and just sleep. But that was a luxury I couldn't afford. I continued to wait, and when my turn came to speak to the officer at the desk I told him that I wanted to press charges against my brothers.

'Do you really want to go there?' he said. 'These are your brothers.'

'I'm sorry,' I said, 'but homophobic abuse is a hate crime, and regardless of whether it's a stranger on the street or a member of my family, I'm going to report it and press charges.'

The officer sighed and said, 'Go home, think about it, and come back in the morning.'

I went home, thought about it and came back the next morning. 'I want to press charges.'

A few years earlier I had been in the middle of a different kind of mental distress. I could barely talk and my life was spent in silence and imagined danger. But now I was faced with the possibility of real danger, and my voice had to come through. No word could be wasted. I had to express myself clearly and eloquently and I did.

After I pressed charges my brothers pulled a disappearing act. I realised then that the only way to deal with bullies is to hit them where it hurts: the law. The police treated my case as a hate crime and put me in contact with the Victim Support Unit, who sent a locksmith to reinforce my door. My flat was turned into a fortress. Once that was sorted out I was put in touch with a lawyer, who immediately drafted injunction warnings to my three older siblings. Even though it was mentally and emotionally draining, what was more traumatic was the fact that I was losing my family. I grew up in a very close-knit family where everything was shared, and I was now an outcast in a very real sense.

When I emailed my father to explain the situation I didn't hear back from him. My older sister stopped speaking to me and my younger sister moved out of my flat. After so much progress I was back where I had started: in a state of depression and isolation. The great boon was that I had love in the form of JT and I was now enrolled on the Creative Writing MA programme at Royal Holloway. But the sense of sadness and trauma didn't lift for at least two years.

My doctor often tells me that everything in life is cyclical. I could become unwell again next year or the year after. I could lose loved ones and gain new friends in the process. I had always thought of family as a fixed, all-powerful entity. I was raised in a culture where family was the most important thing. But as a gay man I had to learn that nothing in life is fixed, especially families. And as a gay man I had to learn that I live in a country where I don't have suffer in silence; that there are laws that protect my rights. As a gay man I had to learn in a bittersweet way that I can choose my family, that certain people have come into my life who share a genuine sense of affinity with me. We may not have the power to choose the family we're born into but we can certainly choose the family we decide to make our own.

Interestingly, ever since I distanced myself from my family the voices I used to hear in my head have stopped. I am no longer paranoid. I walk down the street with a sense of optimism and a lack of fear. I lead a happy life now and I realise, with sadness but without regret, that my family were a hindrance to my personal health and happiness. This is not meant as a mean-spirited jibe but as a plain fact. Coming from a conservative family I was taught to repress many things I enjoyed in life, such as jewellery or hair-dye. These things may sound trivial but their symbolic value cannot be overstated.

It is also painful and telling that the voices I heard in my head when I was unwell were always shouting homophobic slurs at me. Those voices didn't belong to strange, nebulous creatures. Those voices belonged to my family.

*

In November 2011, I got a phone call in the middle of the night. The area code indicated that it was from Somalia and I knew who was calling.

'Hello? Diriye?' came my father's voice.

'Hi dad,' I said in a relaxed tone. 'How are you?'

'I'm fine, thank you.'

'Where are you calling from?'

'I'm in Mogadishu at the moment.'

'Nice. What's up?'

'I saw your artwork online and I read somewhere that you've had a difficult life. What is this difficult life you speak of? You've had a good life.'

'Is that why you're calling me?' I sighed.

'Also, Diriye, and this is very important, so please take note. This gay business that you mention is something I don't understand.'

'What don't you understand about it?' I said. 'It should be pretty clear by now.'

'You know, when you told me that you were gay several years ago, I assumed that it was the mental illness speaking.'

My blood pressure started to rise. 'If you genuinely believed that you would have kept in touch.'

'So it's not the mental illness then?'

'No, dad. I'm a gay man who's pretty proud of being a gay man.'

There was silence on the other line.

'You're proud of being gay?'

'Very much so,' I said. 'Coming out was one of the best things that happened to me.'

'This is not our custom. We have a faith. Are you telling me that you're not a Muslim?'

'I am a Muslim but I'm also very gay and I like it.'

'I cannot accept this,' he said, his voice rising.

'That's entirely your business. You gave up your parental rights when you disowned me two years ago. I have my own family now and I don't need you.'

'Please stay away from my kids and stay away from me,' he shouted.

'I don't care for your family and I don't care for you. Two years. Two fucking years. That's how long it takes for you to call me and this is all you have to say for yourself? You're a coward.'

And with that, I hung up.

When faced with unpleasant experiences, I take a breath and listen to calming music. And I pray. Not the prayer that my parents had taught me, that I had been caned and cajoled into repeating when I was younger: this prayer only requires me to close my eyes and allow the thoughts to float around in my head until they turn into colours. It is an act of pleasure, silence, stillness.

I remembered a quote by Audre Lorde that I had once read online and smiled. She had said, 'Your Silence Will Not Protect You.' In honour of that quote I created a little comic strip on my phone and posted it on Facebook that night. I went to bed afterwards tired but undefeated

The comic strip was an image of a toddler knelt in prayer and the caption I placed beneath it read: 'I didn't know I was here. But I am now. There's beauty in grace. I will continue to dream wide awake. I will continue to soar.'

المرأة الأخرى

THE OTHER (WO)MAN

'Freedom is what you do with what's been done to you.'

– SARTRE

he first thing that struck Yassin on joining Gaydar was the number of men who claimed to be in search of meaningful relationships but were more than happy to settle for meaningless sex. Members' profiles would mention their fondness for opera or ballet but would then undermine the effect by adding details of their ideal lovers' anatomical require-ments: 'XVWE a +', for instance, which Yassin eventually decoded as, 'Extra Very Well-Endowed a Plus'.

The site ran a competition to determine the sex appeal of its members called 'Sex Factor'. The winners were typically men who exhibited considerable muscle-mass and had the words 'straight-acting' as part of their profiles. Feminine-acting men, Yassin soon noticed, were considered losers. Manliness was the thing most worth embodying, even if that manliness was a front, hence the term 'straight-*acting*'.

This was dispiriting. Yassin was a slightly feminine young man who, no less than the others, desired the ideal male as presented in underwear ads: a man so sculpted as to seem super-real. He worshipped musculature, and for someone shy like himself Gaydar seemed the best place to find it. Here was a world in which youth and a lack of sexual inhibition were valuable currency. Yassin was inhibited, but he was at least young.

The chat-rooms were always empty but the cruising rooms would often be packed with men in hard-core bartering mode: 'Fit athletic fucker in Holborn. Private message me pls!' would read one ad, whilst another would say, 'Hung sex-bomb that will blow you up! Can accommodate in WC1. Private message please!' Nearly every ad would end on a forceful, pleading note.

Yassin posted the following on his profile page:

Hi, I'm a young African art student living and study-ing in South London. When I'm not studying, I enjoy listening to anything that has a rhythm that makes my heart want to dance. I'm smooth, passive (only in the sense of 'under the sheets') and would love to meet men with flavour, a great attitude, who love life, art and everything in between. If you fit the bill, feel free to hit me up.

He sat back, pleased. He did not, however, attach a picture. A myriad of reasons against doing so filled his head, both generic (someone crazy recognising him from it and attacking him on the street) and specific to him, a Somali Muslim not so long arrived in London.

After three months of fruitless waiting for suitable responses Yassin decided to cancel his account with Gaydar and venture out into the real world, even though a different set of terrifying rules applied to dating beyond cyberspace. He hated the fact that his physical urges could control his every thought, every dream, and that a need for release had begun to dominate all other im-pulses. When he awoke he often found his sheets damp and stained.

On the night that he decided to close his Gaydar ac-count he found a message in his inbox. Even though he was still determined to close the account, curiosity got the better of him and he opened the message. It read:

Hey,

I really like your profile. There's a youthful joie de vivre about your whole demeanour that I find attractive. My name is Jude and I work as a pilot in the army (not as intriguing as it sounds).

In the rare time that I have to myself I love playing jazz standards on my guitar, reading African literature (Soyinka and Habila are two of my favourites – the Nigerians always do it best, don't they?) and generally relaxing. What's your name and what do you do for work and pleasure?

Deepest regards,
Jude x

The message was charming but Yassin was wary. Why would a self-assured man such as Jude seemed to be find him attractive unless he had some hidden defect? Yassin thought it unlikely that someone who pushed all his buttons would fancy him as well, on the Sod's Law principle if nothing deeper. He chain-smoked several Sovereign cigarettes to calm himself down, then opened the pictures Jude had attached to the email.

There were four of them: a collage of the man Jude wanted to present himself as being. Here he was in his army accoutrements, brows furrowed, looking into the distance as a helicopter hovered above him. Here he was in a scuba-diving suit, displaying an enviable physique while standing on the deck of a yacht. And here he was again, wearing a fedora, dashiki and no shoes whilst strumming a guitar in a bar. The final picture was a full portrait, and in this image he looked at the camera in a warm manner that suggested the photographer was an old lover. The images seemed so orchestrated they were like advertisements for life in the army. All that was missing was a slogan like 'Be All You Can Be.'

Despite that, Yassin found himself imagining being held in those arms. He imagined kissing those lips. Even though Jude's body was youthfully athletic, his face looked much older, like he was in his late forties. Yassin was uncertain about this. He was only twenty-two himself and felt intimidated by the age difference between them. He liked the idea of a more experienced lover but not one who would use his greater experience to try and dominate him in ways he didn't want to be dominated. Yassin continued scanning the images as if for hidden information. The more he examined them the more he began to see flaws: compact became short; skin like melted chocolate was greasy. Jude had droopy eyelids, which made him seem bored with life. His salt-and-pepper crew-cut glistened with beads of oil whilst his teeth seemed unnaturally white and straight – like small Chiclets planted in perfect rows inside the contours of his mouth.

Without realising it Yassin had begun to convince himself that Jude was unattractive, even though, viewed without the distorting lens of self-doubt through which Yassin saw the world, that was obviously not the case. He had scrutinised the pictures with the ruthlessness of a forensic scientist until Jude broke up into a pixelated blur of pure unseemliness. But when he looked at the pictures again he noticed Jude's sculpted cheekbones, his eyebrows that lifted like a seagull's wings.

So he replied to Jude's message and said,

Hi Jude,

Lovely to e-meet you. Thank you for your kind words. Compliments will get you places! ☺ I'm a student at Lewisham College where I'm undertaking a diploma in Art and Design. It's really tedious to be honest. The teachers are full of the gas and the whole atmosphere is dry as hell. But I'm hoping to complete this course so I can apply to Camberwell College of Art and Design and study fine art.

Your job sounds fascinating even though there must be the constant fear of being posted out to Iraq or Afghanistan. It would be nice to meet up sometime if you're up for it. Drop me a text or give me a buzz on 079 4568 3452. It would be cool to hear from you.

Peace out,
Yass

After sending the message Yassin sat and waited for a reply. None came, even though the icon indicated that Jude was online. After a while, mildly disappointed, Yassin logged off and ventured into his tiny kitchen to cook dinner. Around fifteen minutes later his mobile rang. He picked it up awkwardly with greasy hands.

'Hi, is this Yass?' asked a mellifluous baritone voice.

'The one and only,' said Yassin, sudden excitement tugging at his chest. 'Who dis and what can I do you for?'

'Hi, it's Jude from online. I hope I'm not calling at a bad time.'

'Nah, mon plaisir. I was just making dinner: macaroni and cheese. So calorific it's coma-inducing!'

'Aah, my kinda guy,' Jude said. His voice had a slight Jamaican lilt. 'A brother who eats heartily is a beautiful thing.'

'Are you taking the piss?' Yassin replied cheerily. 'So you want me to die of a stroke brought on by a fatty diet? I thought you were more of a sofisticato.'

'No, I'm just a middle-aged ragamuffin who loves his junk food.'

'Well, it's so tempting to gorge on a greasy kebab even when you feel you've got to maintain a relatively decent figure. Though, I must say, rather ashamedly, that I'm part of the brigade that loves athletic, toned men. It's shallow but true. '

'So would you have replied to my message if I was fat?' asked Jude.

'I would,' said Yassin, 'But I don't know about attraction. I have to admit I do like my men fit and masculine.'

'Oh, that's such a cliché! I like my men with curvy bodies and feminine characteristics.'

'Well, you're in luck. I happen to be such a bredda.'

'I couldn't tell because you hadn't posted up any photos,' said Jude, 'but I loved your message. It just seemed so happy and playful.'

'I don't know about that, but muchos gracias for the compliments, señor.'

'You're most welcome, sir,' said Jude, 'are you smooth?'

'Silken,' smiled Yassin, 'soft as talcum powder. Why? What are your intentions with me?'

'To turn you on,' whispered Jude. 'Make you sing arias while I stroke you.'

At this Yassin laughed. 'You're bluffing. You can't be *that* good.'

'Why don't you try me? Say tomorrow evening? I'll show you what I'm all about.'

'That's dope,' said Yassin. 'But you seem to have forgotten one of the tenets of dating etiquette, which is to tell me a little bit more about yourself.'

'Well, I'm forty-eight years old, British Jamaican. My army base is in Oxford and it's a job I've had for the last twenty years. I've been married for eighteen of those years.'

'Oh,' said Yassin. 'And are you still married?' What did he want from him if he was married? 'Do you have any kids?'

'Yes and yes,' said Jude quietly. 'I have a son and a daughter, who are thirteen and fifteen...'

'I see,' was all Yassin could say. 'Thank you for your honesty. I suppose a lot of men would have lied about it.'

Rain began to beat against the kitchen window. Just as Yassin was considering hanging up on him Jude said quickly, 'To be honest, Yass, my marriage has been an unhappy one for years. My wife Erika and I are only together for our kids. She knows I hook up with other men, and even though she was angry at first, she couldn't care less now. I'm telling you these things because I wanted to be upfront about my situation. I like you. I think you're cool and sexy and I think we'd be great together. What do you say? At least let me take you out for dinner tomorrow night. Come on, what do you say?'

'Oh, I don't know – ' said Yassin.

'Don't make me beg, Yass. Please don't make me beg!' Jude chuckled in an embarrassed way.

'No,' Yassin said, reaching a decision. 'I won't make you beg. Meet me at eight inside the Petitou café in Peckham.' Yassin gave Jude the address and added, 'Don't be late.'

'I won't,' said Jude, 'I'll see you then, beautiful.'

After Yassin had hung up the phone he sat quietly in his living-room, listening to the rain patter against the windows.

*

'So you think I'm making a mistake?' Yassin asked, passing a cigarette to his friend Savannah.

'*Duh!*' she replied.   They were sitting on the front steps of the college. It was lunchtime and the majority of the student body had gathered outside to gossip over tobacco or weed. The young lads in their hoodies flirted with pretty girls in tight jeans with the words 'princess' and 'diva' emblazoned across their buttocks, and the security guards looked on as weed-smoke clouded the air. Theoretically the college had a strict No Drugs policy but the guards, tired of chasing after kids who didn't feel the slightest bit intimidated by their presence, now ignored the scenes of drug-abuse that unfolded on their watch.

'Honey, it's not difficult to see through this guy's non-sense,' Savannah went on, puffing away at Yassin's Sovereign. 'He wants to maintain his relationship with his wife, come home to a good meal, spend quality time with his kids, which is fair enough. But he also wants to use you as a receptacle for the sexual fantasies his wife can't fulfil. This fucker wants to have his cake and not only eat it but *gorge* on it!'

Savannah was a self-confessed 'straight-talking, plus-size rude gyal who happens to like women.' She had a shaved head and a distaste for bullshit. Having taken a few short courses in counselling before transferring to Yassin's art course she prided herself on being an expert in analysing people, Freud reincarnated as a barb-hurling black lesbian.

'I say ditch the djam fool and find yourself a man with high morals. Or at least *some* morals.'

Yassin was unconvinced. 'Jude may seem like an arse on paper,' he said. 'But he's a really nice guy.'

Savannah snorted.

'At least he was honest.'

'What's going to happen if his wife finds out? Put yourself in her shoes. I know you want a relationship but this half-life mess isn't the way to go about it.'

Yassin sighed, recalling the image he had had of London when he lived in Kenya as a place teeming with romantic possibilities, where he would never have to worry about being alone again. In Somalia and Kenya, the countries he was born and raised in respectively, homosexuality was something to be hidden for fear of violence. The chances of meeting other men like him were slim and so he quietly buried his desire and prayed for the day he could leave for England. After immigrating to London he had slowly allowed the mask to slip as he became more comfortable in his new surroundings. But despite the city's myriad possibilities here he was, four years later, lonelier than ever.

He thought about the thousands of men on sites like Gaydar, huddled miserably over their computers, desperate to connect, and realised that London's scale only deepened the isolation he felt; magnified it and made it unbearable. That was how come an affair with a married man twice his age could seem like a golden opportunity. He finished the cigarette.

Petitou was an organic café in Peckham's bohemian quarter. It was tucked away in the suburb of Bellenden village, which was a far cry from the rest of Peckham. A few metres away from the crowded, run-down high street with its Poundlands and discount shops, this area had a more affluent feel to it. It was here one could find owner-run boutiques and independent bookshops, organic food-stores and chocolate cafés. It was a well-managed island around which the rest of Peckham swirled chaotically. A few minutes down the same road from Petitou one could find rotten fruit and vegetable-peelings from the market littered across the street. One could hear an imam's call to prayer at the local mosque or high-life blaring from Nigerian barbershops. There was a startling contrast between poor minorities and rich white folks, and even though the physical distance between their worlds was small, that proximity only served to emphasize the larger social and cultural divisions between them.

Yassin arrived at the café ten minutes early and found a corner to sit in. The place was filled with white women and their expensive push-chairs, and for a moment he wondered if he had chosen the right place for a first date. He caught his reflection in the glass of the table and wondered whether he had put too much Brylcreem in his hair. He ordered a glass of orange juice and sat quietly in his corner, poring over the menu. As forks clinked against plates African muzak played softly in the background, making his mind drift. As Yassin daydreamed the door opened and a man carrying a curious-looking plant walked in. Yassin immediately recognised Jude. He was wearing an army camouflage jacket, and was shorter and beefier than Yassin had expected. Jude saw him and flashed his set of beautiful teeth before walking over.

'Hey Jude,' said Yassin standing up to shake his hand.

'Ah, the remarkable Yass,' said Jude. 'What a pleasure to finally meet you.'

'I see you got lost in the Amazon on your way here,' smiled Yassin, motioning to the plant, which was about a foot tall, a bundle of tubes that rose from green into a beautiful shade of red.

'It's for you.'

'It looks like something from *The Little Shop of Horrors!*'

'Well, my friend,' smiled Jude, pulling up a chair and sitting down next to him, 'this is a pitcher plant. It feeds off insects that get lured in and trapped inside its cavities. I wanted to get you something unique so you'd always remember our first date. I didn't think flowers would've done the trick.'

'How do you know that flowers *wouldn't* have done

the trick?' said Yassin. 'I'm very easy to please.'

'Well, you say that now, but I doubt that you are. You seem like a man - '

'Who demands shit?' interrupted Yassin, laughing. 'I hardly think so! But it's great that you have this impression of me as someone who plays hardball.'

'I don't know,' said Jude, looking at him flirtatiously. 'You just seem like a man who knows what he wants.'

'Well, I won't stop you there, homeboy. Keep the compliments coming!'

It was Jude's turn to laugh, and as he did so he ran his hands softly over Yassin's under the table. They were rough and calloused but Yassin loved the feel of them. These were hands that had done manual labour. It was a long time since he had been touched in this way.

'I love your smile.'

'Thanks,' said Jude slightly self-consciously. 'They're not my real teeth. I lost them in the Gulf War.'

'Oh, I'm really sorry to hear that,' said Yassin.

'These things happen,' shrugged Jude. 'Besides, these new implants make me look a million times better than before.'

'Why? Were you a gargoyle?' chuckled Yassin.

'That's right, people,' said Jude, motioning good-naturedly to the other diners. 'We have a regular comedian in the house tonight!'

'Hey, I'm just teasing.'

'I know, gorgeous. I can tease too!'

'Okay, serious question now,' said Yassin. 'But you definitely don't have to answer it if you don't want to.'

'Okay, shoot.'

'Funny you should say that. Have you ever actually shot or killed anyone whilst on duty?'

Jude looked slightly irritated by the question. After a long beat he said, 'Yeah,' rather flatly, then allowed the silence to drag.

Diriye Osman

'Hey,' said Yassin, feeling his voice rise, 'let's order something. This place does the most amazing quiches.'

'Yes, let's,' said Jude, looking relieved.

They ordered quiche and smoked salmon, along with a bottle of Merlot. As Yassin tucked into his meal Jude said, 'Tell me a little bit more about yourself. Where're you from originally?'

'Ah, the heritage question,' smiled Yassin, taking a sip of his wine. 'I was born in Somalia but moved to Kenya after the civil war broke out and lived there until I was eighteen. I'm now twenty-two.'

'So young, so green,' smirked Jude.

"So young' I'll agree with, but not so sure about 'so green'. I'd like to think I'm relatively experienced.'

'What was life like in Kenya?'

'It was... interesting,' said Yassin evasively. He remembered the scent of Omo detergent and the taste of steaming rice with maharagwe – red beans. He remembered the mango, pawpaw and banana trees that grew in his family's garden. He remembered the fireflies that sparkled like fairy dust on warm nights. He remembered the police raiding his compound in search of Somali refugees. He remembered hiding in closets as a child to avoid getting deported. He remembered his stepmother Fartun trying desperately to quieten his younger sister Lul whenever the police banged on their door looking for kipandas - legal papers - or kitu kidogo – 'something small' – for 'tea'. He remembered his father showing him pictures of his birth-mother whilst Fartun went into the next room and wept about the fact that she could never compete with a dead woman's memory. He remembered having a massive fight with Fartun one evening, telling her she would never be his mother and she, looking to hurt him the way he had hurt her, shouting, 'If your mother had raised you, you would have turned out a faggot!' The irony of course was that it was Fartun who had raised him and he still turned out a faggot.

Yassin sighed.

'I lived in this sleepy suburb in Nairobi with my family,' he said. 'My father owned a fishery in Mombasa and my stepmother was a housewife. I grew up with my two siblings, Nasra and Lul. The family are planning to move to London next year since my father's business has gone bust. They're also moving because Kenya has become an increasingly hostile place for Somalis to live.'

'So I guess they'll be all up in your business?'

'I hope not,' said Yassin.

'Well I hope it works out for you,' said Jude, raising his glass. 'To personal freedom.'

'To personal freedom,' toasted Yassin. 'Do you want to come back to mine after this?'

Jude flashed his beautiful smile. 'I'd like that very much.'

They rushed through the rest of the meal, paid the bill and stepped out of the café into the cold winter night.

'The bus-stop is just around the corner,' said Yassin.

Jude fished in his pockets and extracted a key fob. He pressed the unlocker and flash went the lights of a sleek black Range Rover parked outside the café.

'Who said anything about taking the bus?'

'Good-looking ride,' said Yassin as Jude opened the door for him.

'Not as good-looking as the guy sitting next to me,' smiled Jude as he started the engine. A jaunty Eighties electro track burst out of the speakers. The singer was Grace Jones, snarling her way through the song in her menacing contralto like a pugilist sensing blood.

'This is my 'choon!' said Jude as he pulled out. '*Demolition Man* is such a 'choon. You like Grace Jones?'

'I can't say that I do,' said Yassin.

'I'll make you a mix-tape and I promise you'll love it.'

'I'm sure I will. Why don't you mail me the tracks as

mp3 files?'

'Mate, I don't do mp3s! If I can't smell the vinyl or feel its texture, I ain't buying it. Your generation is moving too fast for its own good. Soon you'll hear about people having sex wearing oxygen masks. You've got to have the human element.'

'Whatever, man,' said Yassin. 'Just give the mix-tape to me in any format. I'm breezy like that.'

Yassin's estate was an ugly mass of greyness and rot. Outside the windows of each flat deteriorated drainage pipes dripped nastiness onto the heads of pedestrians passing below. The buildings were about to be demolished and most of the tenants had been relocated, leaving the majority of the flats boarded up. Yassin's rent was low, but the place was a breeding-ground for thugs, drug-dealers and waste-cadets.

A few months earlier a Nigerian couple had thrown a party in their flat to celebrate the birth of their new baby. Two armed thugs broke down their door and busted in. The thugs demanded beer, and the husband was more than willing to give it to them, along with anything else they wanted, as long as they left his family and guests unharmed. The wife, holding her newborn baby, emboldened by new parenthood, refused to accept their demands. Without missing a beat one of the thugs raised his gun and shot her straight through the skull: a bullseye of blood and nerve tissue. The woman toppled in such a way that the baby was unharmed. She had held onto her child even in death. That night Yassin couldn't sleep from the wails and screams reverberating around the estate.

'Is this where you live?' asked Jude in disbelief as he turned into the parking lot.

'Unfortunately,' said Yassin.

'Shit, Yass I like you and ting but I'd be properly vexed if my car was tiefed or torched. This area looks *rough*!'

'Don't worry about it, man,' said Yassin. 'They'll just jack your fly rims, your expensive system. Hell, they might even tief your leather seats!'

'I'm serious, Yass! This car cost me a year's salary!'

'Look, it won't get jacked,' said Yassin. 'Let's just park the car on a safer street not too far away.'

They drove the Range into a quiet residential street not far from where Yassin lived. Then they walked back to the estate and climbed the four flights of stairs to get to Yassin's flat.

'Welcome to my extremely humble abode,' said Yassin, ushering Jude in ahead of him.

'Hmm,' said Jude, as he entered the flat, admiring the African prints adorning the walls in the hall. 'You take your heritage pretty seriously.'

'I try to,' said Yassin, taking Jude's coat as they passed into the lounge and placing it on the sofa. 'I just wanted to give this place a lickle flavour, you know?

'Styling,' said Jude, looking at the paintings on the walls of the lounge, a series of colourful images of black men in sensuous poses. Jude traced his fingers along them. 'It's almost as if they have a 3D effect. Did you paint them?'

'Yes,' said Yassin. 'I initially did them as an art project but the pictures were too risqué to submit so I just said, 'fuck it, I'm going to hang them on my wall."

'What did you do instead?'

'Some paintings of Maasai herdsmen. My tutors lapped that shit right up. The British love the exotic.'

'But to a Maasai herdsman he's just doing business as usual. Didn't all this seem exotic to you when you first came here?

'It's true,' said Yassin, sliding an Aaliyah CD into the stereo. 'But I've learnt that when it comes to being an African artist working in a white field, tutors or patrons want my experiences to reflect their fantasies: the clichéd notion of the noble savage. Sometimes you have to give in, because they hold your destiny in their hands.'

'But isn't that a cop-out?' asked Jude.

'It's reality.'

'Hmm.'

Jude bent forward and kissed him on the lips. It was a tentative kiss; soft, delicate. Yassin traced the tip of Jude's tongue with his own. It tasted of wine. He then kissed Jude harder, darting his tongue in and out of Jude's mouth. The incense-smoke in the room, the airy falsetto of Aaliyah seeping from the stereo: R&B's answer to the Kama Sutra.

Yassin slid onto Jude's lap and gyrated slowly on his crotch, feeling him harden. They rocked each other's boats like this for a while, their bodies moving in a sweaty rhythm. Yassin's body melted like wax. Jude then unzipped Yassin's fly and pulled down his jeans and underwear, turning him around so he could taste him. He did so with circular motions of his tongue, opening him up gradually and then spreading him wide. Aaliyah chanted suggestively in the background, urging them on.

As Yassin was on the verge of orgasm, Jude said something that made him lie awake in bed all night.

'The man said he wanted to fuck your *pussy!*' screamed Savannah.

'Ssh!' said Yassin, glancing around him at the other students idling on the college steps. 'Yes, but what does it mean?'

'He's trying to emasculate you. This guy wants a man who's feminine enough to take over his wife's position but is a man and so doesn't have to be cared for. That way he has the best of both worlds.'

'Oh, well,' Yassin said. 'I'm not going to write him off just because he made a gaffe during sex. In fact, I'm seeing him again tomorrow.'

'What about the pitcher plant?' said Savannah, 'The fucker gave you a plant that *eats* things on a first date! What does that say about him?'

'That he's original?' said Yassin, blowing smoke out of his nose. 'I like this guy. He's a little off-beat and flawed but that's part of his allure.'

'I'm just saying be careful, Yass. This guy gives me negative vibrations.'

'Sav, the whole world gives you negative vibrations! And the plant eats flies. That's a good thing, isn't it?'

The next evening Jude came over to Yassin's flat. He smelt like mint and Egoiste and he was carrying a carrier bag from La Senza. He sank onto the couch, pulled Yassin to him and started kissing him hungrily.

'Is that a gift to appease the wife?' asked Yassin, breaking off the kiss and indicating the lingerie bag.

'Actually, it's for you,' said Jude, passing the bag over to him.

'I didn't know La Senza did men's underwear,' said Yassin.

'Open it,' said Jude, grazing Yassin's neck with his lips. Yassin opened the bag and took out a pair of silk stockings. He looked quizzically at Jude.

'I want you to try them on,' purred Jude, nuzzling Yassin's ear.

'Why?'

'I know you're not used to them, but once you try them on you're going to love them. Go on, try them.'

'So now you want me to dress like a woman for you?' Yassin said, standing up abruptly. 'I'm sorry, Jude, but I'm gay not a tranny, and there is a big fucking difference.'

'Hey, calm down,' said Jude. 'I just thought it'd be a bit of fun.'

'A bit of fun?' shouted Yassin, 'You want to turn me

into a fucking woman. You don't want a man and you
certainly don't want a woman. You just want someone in
between who you can foist your fantasies on. Well, that's
not me, alright? You need to get the fuck out of my
house!'

'Yass, if you would let me explain,' said Jude.

'Out!' shouted Yassin.

Jude picked up his jacket and crossed to the front
door slowly, as if expecting Yassin to change his mind.
But that didn't happen and Yassin slammed the door in
his face. After knocking quietly on the door for a few
minutes, Jude shuffled away. When Jude's footfalls on
the stairs had faded away, Yassin sat on the floor and
quietly wiped tears from his face.

Yassin spent the next few days in his flat, avoiding
everyone, his life suspended in chaos, until the whole
place reeked of stale cigarette smoke, Indian takeaways
and overflowing rubbish bins. There were moments he
wanted to call Savannah and tell her what had happened.
Jude rang repeatedly. There were times Yassin wanted to
pick up and listen to his side of the story.

On the fourth day of his self-imposed retreat he decided that he needed fresh air and went out for a walk. A
group of teenage boys were smoking weed in his building's stairwell. Usually Yassin would have felt uneasy
about passing by them but today he couldn't care less. He
headed towards Peckham Rye. He saw men with their
wives and girlfriends and wondered if they were cheating
on them with other men. It began to rain. He put up his
hood.

As he walked without a goal he wondered whether he
had strayed so far from his own roots that there was no
going back. He wondered what going back could even
mean. He came from a community that lived by strict
Islamic rules and here he was beyond even the periphery

of that culture, so much so that he had had to create his own rules as he went along. He felt his sense of Somaliness slipping away from him and he was afraid of letting it go, afraid of the moral, psychological and social anarchy its loss threatened to create within him. But at the same time, what was he really hanging onto? A sense of social allegiance? But wouldn't he be automatically excluded from his community because of his sexual orientation wherever his own allegiance lay? He didn't belong to just one society: he was gay, Somali, Muslim, and yet all these cultural positions left him excluded. It was Somaliness, the pure beauty of being part of a proud, distinctive culture, that glued all his other selves together. He was Somali first, Muslim second, gay third. But perhaps that hierarchy was only a matter of timing: born Somali, raised Muslim, discovered gay. And now he was venturing out into the world without a sense of his place within it and this frightened him. Yet he realised that he couldn't mourn what was lost but instead had to consider what was to be gained. He knew he would never belong but did he really want to? To deny one aspect of himself for another?

It was now raining so hard that his hoodie was sodden and his whole body was quivering with cold, but he continued on down Peckham Rye, oblivious to the world outside his head. He needed release, and suddenly he thought the best way to achieve this would be to run. So he ran past the crowds on Peckham Rye, ran like his life depended on it. He ran until his heart was in his mouth, until he felt dizzy and sick. When he couldn't run anymore, when he had gone as far as his stamina and his need could take him, he stumbled to a stop outside a halal butchers. The smell of blood and beef filled his nostrils. He couldn't even remember the last time he ate halal meat. Did that make him even more of a heathen?

Out of breath and nauseous, for a moment he thought

he was going to throw up on the pavement. His body felt weak and exhausted. It was as if he had been running towards something, a sense of freedom perhaps, but had failed to find it on Peckham Rye. He tried to catch his breath. He turned and slowly started back towards his home. The distance felt long and difficult, a journey in a fairytale, with home the closest thing to heaven he could think of. As he turned towards Queen's Road he saw a minicab office and outside it, sheltering under a sagging and grimy candy-striped awning, stood a group of Somali cab-drivers. They were chewing khat, the leafy drug that has the same effect on the body as speed, yet they looked old and tired. Yassin looked at these men for a few moments, him standing on one side of the street, them on the other, and felt a great divide between them. Yet when he looked at their faces, worn by worry and depression, he was reminded that his people were a traumatised community who didn't realise they were traumatised: by war, dislocation, poverty, miseducation and a genera-tional rift between young and old; by the tear between the past and the future. It was a kind of collective psychosis, each sufferer oblivious to the fact that they were paying for the sins of their fathers and their father's fathers, caught in a perpetual arrested development. Yassin would not make the same mistakes they had made. He would hack out his own place in the world. He would drive out his demons and achieve happiness. He would find other ways of being.

That evening Yassin sat on his bed and examined the stockings Jude had given him. He had to admit they were beautiful. He studied the golden seams and enjoyed the liquid texture of the silk against his fingers. Would it be such a terrible thing to try them on? Without thinking about it further he removed his trousers and slid the stockings on, rolling them up carefully to slip them past his bare, pointed toes without laddering them as he had seen his sisters do. They felt wonderful against his skin. He stood and posed in front of the mirror. He felt unexpectedly natural as he tiptoed around the room. He recalled the heavenly creatures he had seen in the fashion magazines, the lithe modelas, and for the first time he felt like them: gorgeous, uninhibited, self-assured. He sashayed around the room as if wearing high heels and imagined himself on a catwalk in Paris or Milan, striking a pose for the paparazzi. He felt free in those stockings, freer than he had felt in a long time. He now understood why some men dressed this way: it allowed them to become for a short private while the heavenly creatures in their heads, the beautiful girls who had the world in their palms.

As Yassin strutted in his stockings, he knew that things would never be the same.

'Thank you so much for getting back to me,' said Jude as he entered Yassin's flat. 'I was wrong to push my fetishes on you. I'm sorry.'

His eyes looked tired and his hair was grown out and looked natty. He was wearing his army camouflage outfit as if he had come straight from the military base where he was stationed. He no longer smelt fragrant and instead a hint of body odour emanated from him. He looked as if he hadn't slept properly.

Yassin greeted him wearing a long bathrobe and a pair of slippers. 'Come on in and take a seat. And don't worry about what happened. It's your thing, you like transvestites. I'm not sure if I constitute as one but...'

As Jude sat on the couch Yassin let the bathrobe fall to the ground. He was wearing nothing but the stockings underneath. His skin was fine as a feather and he parted his legs whilst standing on the tips of his toes the way he had seen the models pose.

'Wow!' said Jude, pulling him close and kissing him softly on his pubic bone. 'You look like a dream.' He took Yassin's rapidly-stiffening penis deep into his mouth until Yassin's knees were about to give. Jude then turned him around and rimmed him. Then Yassin undressed Jude, almost tearing the buttons off his uniform. Jude's pectorals and abs shimmered with sweat like moist cobblestones. His thighs were muscular and strongly defined and Yassin kissed them. Jude's muscles loosened with each touch as if Yassin's lips were weed-smoke: unfiltered dopeness. They held each other tightly to satiate the physical ache they both felt, as if they were afraid to let go, afraid of what letting go would mean.

'I want you inside me,' said Jude, kissing Yassin's neck.

'Really?' said Yassin, 'Why?'

'I've always had a fantasy about a man in drag doing me.'

'I don't know about that,' said Yassin. 'You're the active one.'

'Please do this for me. I promise you the most sensuous time of your life.'

Reluctantly Yassin agreed. It was one thing for a man to fuck a transvestite, but it put a bizarre twist to things for a passive, would-be transvestite to fuck a masculine, active man. Still, a part of him was curious. Yassin lubricated Jude and spread his legs wide. He fumbled on a condom with slick, uncertain fingers, pushed in and tentatively began to stroke him. It was as if someone else was having sex instead of him. He felt slightly repulsed by it all and tried to remain hard as he moved his hips back and forth. He noticed a bluebottle buzzing around the room. He kept his eyes on it, tuning out Jude's moans. It hovered close to the pitcher plant, which was sitting on the coffee-table, then came to a rest on the curving lip of one of the pitchers. It moved around curiously, turned this way and that, then tumbled down inside. Jude groaned louder. As Yassin fucked him all he could hear was the bluebottle buzzing for survival inside the plant's cavities.

After they were done Yassin handed Jude back his plant and stockings and saw him to the door.

After a sleepless night he called Savannah first thing in the morning to relay the latest news.

'Good riddance to the djam blood-clot!" she said, a bit too chirpily. 'Come out with me to this dope dyke bar tonight, hon. No men on the down-low, no tranny-fuckers; just soulful sisters and sexy music. You'll love it.'

So Yassin was heading to Primark to treat himself to a new shirt for the evening in the hopes that it would lift his spirits. While he was waiting to cross the road two buses passed by in different directions, on each one a slogan. The first read: 'There probably is no God. So stop worry-ing and enjoy your life.' Whilst the second one stated, 'There definitely is a God. So join the Christian Party and enjoy your life.' Yassin sighed and wandered into Pri-mark. The store was packed with crash-strapped folks fishing for bargains: Jamaican girls barely fifteen pushing prams whilst flicking through racks of £2 padded bras that would make them seem older; Somali men with greasy hair trying out £10 jackets for snapshots to send back home, to prove that they were living the high life in the West.

Yassin crossed to the men's section and flicked ab-sent-mindedly through the tee-shirts and vests. Every-thing was banal and leached of colour. He sighed again. As he turned to leave, a glint of light from a sparkling object in the women's section caught his eye.

It was a chunky necklace in the shape of Nefertiti, carved from wood and spray-painted with glitter. It was, he knew, mass-produced, presumably by some sweatshop factory in China, and had never been near Egypt, but at that moment for some strange reason it was one of the most beautiful things he had ever seen. Immediately his heart began to pound. If he bought this necklace would any of the other customers react? Would they shout abuse at him? But then he could say that it was for his wife, his sister, his mother. In his mind he had already begun to create entire characters and fictions in order to permit himself to buy the necklace. He walked tremblingly back to the entrance where the shopping baskets were piled high, picked one up and stuffed the necklace into it. Of course nobody batted an eyelid or even noticed his presence.

Seeing that no-one actually cared about what the hell he bought, he felt emboldened to go deeper into the women's section. At this point his face was burning up with shame and he wanted nothing more than to hide. But he walked over to the padded bra section, grabbed the flimsiest one his eyes could see and, without even checking the size, nonchalantly put it in his basket: he had ventured too far to leave empty-handed. Then he scanned the less-embarrassing scarf section and instinctively reached for the most colourful one – a blend of gold and turquoise. He wanted to try out jeans and tops too, but knew that was too risky, too self-revealing, so instead he called over to a female sales assistant.

'Hi,' he smiled sweetly, 'I have a twin sister and our birthday is next week. I wanted to surprise her by getting her some clothes. I know her style very well and because we're identical, she's exactly my height, my foot size, everything about us is the same except the parts that really matter!' At this point he let out a nervous chuckle whilst the saleswoman smirked in a knowing-but-couldn't-give-a-toss way.

'So you want me to help you find clothes for your 'twin' sister?' she said, as if his transparency was nothing new to her.

'Yes! Could you help me? I'm completely lost here. I wanted to buy her shoes and jeans, a nice blouse even, but just don't know how to convert men and women's sizes.'

'Follow me,' she said drily.

She led him into the jeans section and looked him over. 'I'd say you're a size 34 waist and 32 leg, so – ' She flicked through the jean rack, removed a pair and tossed them at him. 'How about those?'

They were deep blue, cut to fit tightly, with golden butterfly embroidery on the back pockets. 'Perfect!' said Yassin, and put them in the basket. 'Now I need shoes. I like those red pumps with the golden heels.'

The shop-girl cocked her eyebrow. 'What size are you?'

'42.'

'And your sister's feet are that big?'

'What can I say?' shrugged Yassin. 'We're cut from the same cloth.'

'Next you'll be telling me you're the same person,' murmured the shop-girl in a slightly irritated way. She went into the stockroom and came back with a box of shoes. 'Do you want to try them on?'

'Excuse me?' said Yassin, taking the box from her. 'Maybe you hadn't heard me, they're for my sister.'

'I hope your 'sister' enjoys her new clothes,' she scoffed before heading back to the stockroom.

Yassin dipped his fingers into the shopping-basket and stroked the embroidery on the jeans, the curve of the butterfly's wings, the delicacy of the gold stitching. The women's section in Primark was definitely better than the men's.

Paint is an artist's weapon. With just daubs of colour a painter can expose his internal landscape to the world, make his dreams a tangible truth. Yassin was an artist, or at least an artist-in-training, and he knew his way around paint: how to create the right tone and texture, how to add flavour to the proceedings. On this occasion he was his own canvas and he was going to breathe new life into his body. Artists often say that creating art is like playing God. Yassin felt he was creating himself, bending the pages of the rulebook back until the spine split and the leaves came loose. With a few deft strokes of a brush he hoped to unshackle the person locked in his head who was no longer a slave to social convention.

He sat down to work. He dipped his brush into Iman foundation and shaded it gently and evenly across his dome-shaped forehead, high cheekbones and long neck. It had a lambent quality to it that made him seem lit from within. He then applied Kohl around his slanted eyes until he resembled a mahogany china doll. Once that was done he pencilled his thin eyebrows, shading and toning each curve until he looked completely authentic. He moisturised his body with Mango Shea, which made him smell like a fruit cocktail, then sprayed Narciso Rodriguez's For Her across his chest. The last touch was to apply red lipstick to his full lips. He looked and smelt fresh, fly and completely funkdafied.

It was time to put on the clothes. Because he had a curvaceous upper body he didn't need to pad his bra to create an authentic look. He simply clasped the bra tightly and pushed the meat around his chest upwards until it looked like he had cleavage. Pleased with the results, he then tried to get into the butterfly jeans and discovered that they weren't built for a man's crotch. So he tucked his penis and balls in between his legs and taped them in place with masking tape. He had seen that procedure performed in *Paris is Burning,* the cult Eighties film about New York's drag ball culture. Even though he had always loved the film's depiction of drag as gender performance, he had never imagined that it would one day inspire him in his exploration of his own gender role. To wear the jeans was a painful process that went beyond physical discomfort, as if he was neutering himself by camouflaging his manhood in that masochistic way. He felt empowered by the makeup and the tight clothes, as if these social constructions were markers of authentic womanhood.

For this night at least he was willing to erase his male persona and squeeze into the butterfly jeans and tight blouse to complete his transformation into a (wo)man. After that he wiggled into the painful heels, and finally wrapped the scarf around his head and neck like a hijab. He didn't just want to become a (wo)man, he wanted to become a Muslim (wo)man, or at least his playful idea of a Muslim (wo)man. It was ironic that for all his wanting to break free of social strictures he should choose to wear a garment that embodied the very essence of fitting into the mould. He felt that since he was a Muslim he would retain the most conspicuous marker for women of his faith but use it for his own subversive ends. So within his deviation there was a desire to belong to his own tradition although this tradition stipulated that it was sinful to engage in such a deviation. The idea of even questioning one's own gender-role was considered un-Islamic, and here he was, not only questioning it but challenging it in the most dangerous way. His neighbourhood was rough, and if he was seen walking the streets dressed as a Muslim transvestite he was afraid that he would be assaulted. So he rang Savannah.

'Sav, I need you to come pick me up please.'

'Again? Yass, I've picked you up every time we've ever gone out. I suggest you get to my place via the bus.'

'Sav, please. I wouldn't ask if it wasn't important.'

'Yass, what's the deal? Is everything cool?'

'Yes, everything's fine. I just need you to come pick

me up.'

Savannah sighed. 'Alright, I'll be there in a half an hour. Just be ready.'

'Don't worry about that. I'll see you then. And Sav?'

'What?'

'Thanks.'

An hour later Savannah called his mobile. 'I'm outside,' she said.

Yassin grabbed his jacket and left his flat. As he started down the stairs of his building the usual bunch of young men were lounging against the handrail smoking weed, and as he passed them by one of them whistled.

'Hey sexy gyal,' another said, 'where you headed?

'Somewhere you've never been,' said Yassin.

'Ugh!' they chorused in disgusted realisation, 'Batty!'

'No,' said Yassin, 'your *mutha* is batty. I'm simply gay, baby. Roll with the times.' And with that he swept out of the building. He didn't look back for fear of being bottled. He couldn't believe that he had actually insulted the hooligans that hung out on his stairway. Once outside he broke into a run, but in the unfamiliar high heels he soon found himself hobbling.

Savannah's car windows were cloudy with weed-smoke and rare groove was blaring out of her speakers. He stumbled over and knocked hard on her window so that she could unlock the passenger door for him.

'Hurry up, Sav!' he shouted, looking back at the entrance to his building to see if he was being followed by the hooligans. 'Open the fucking door!'

Savannah wound down her window and a cloud of weed-smoke billowed out into the cold air. 'Who the fuck are you?' she said, putting on a defensive screw-face.

'Sav, it's me. Yassin.'

'Fuck *me!*' she shouted. 'Are you *serious?* Get in the car quick!'

Once Yassin was in the car Savannah looked him over

in complete disbelief. 'Oh my Goddess. You look just like a woman. How did you...? *Why* did you...?' Before he could answer, she continued, 'That fucker Jude has succeeded! He's managed to turn you into a tranny; a hot one perhaps but a *fuck*-king tranny nevertheless.'

'Relax, Sav. No one has turned me into anything. I just wanted to see what all the fuss was about.'

'And?' asked Savannah, puffing away at her joint.

'It's incredibly painful,' Yassin laughed. 'But I'm determined to have a good time tonight.'

'Bwoy,' said Savannah, passing him the joint and pulling out of the car park, 'you best be careful looking like that 'cause Goddess knows them dykes will get ideas. You just look too fucking real as a woman; at least 'til you start talking.'

They drove through Dulwich and Herne Hill and down into Brixton. Savannah turned into a backstreet, pulled over and switched off the engine. They sat in the car for a few minutes, smoking in silence. The cooling engine clicked and ticked. Yassin felt as if his body was melting onto the leather seats. He felt sensuous, sexy, powerful.

'Let's groove,' he said, stubbing out the joint.

They walked down the backstreet until they reached a bar called Medusa. A muscular Turkish-looking bouncer blocked the doorway. At the sight of him Yassin's chest tightened with anxiety: in the past he had been either harassed or turned away by bouncers at gay bars, and for a moment he was afraid that this one would do the same. Instead the bouncer stepped aside and ushered them in with a polite, 'Enjoy your evening, ladies.'

'Thank you, darling,' Savannah smiled at him. She wrapped her arm around Yassin's waist and said, 'This is my baby, Yasmeen. Isn't she gorgeous?'

The bouncer nodded appreciatively and asked Yassin, 'Where you from, Yasmeen?'

Diriye Osman

'She's from Somalia,' said Savannah, 'Isn't she just sexy? I bagged myself a Muslim fly gyal!'

'One less for me!' joked the bouncer. Yassin wanted to speak but he was too astonished by the man's reaction. He had never been paid this much attention dressed as a man. Why was he suddenly so lusted over as a woman? Was he that unattractive as a man? In the space of a single evening he had become a performance artist whose female persona had outstripped his male identity in terms of allure. In the masculinity-obsessed world of gay dating his effeminacy was considered unappealing, but when he embraced that effeminacy and became a (wo)man, masculine straight men paid attention. It was a fairytale alternate universe. But like most fairytales, this one had a sting in its tail. If he spoke the spell would be broken.

'Boy, you look good,' chuckled Savannah. 'Even straight men want to fuck you!'

'That bouncer would've run a mile if he knew that 'Yasmeen' had a dick.'

'So what? Say nothing to no-one and just go with the flow.'

As they made their way to the bar Yassin was struck by the difference between the gay clubs he had been to in Soho and Vauxhall, and Medusa. It had a shabby feel to it, unlike most gay clubs, where although most of the men stood around cruising each other or were drugged out of their minds, the sleazy vibe was offset by gleaming decor. Despite Medusa's sagging chairs, murky brown wallpaper and general air of dinginess the women were either engaged in what seemed like relaxed conversation by the bar, or they were dancing to songs like Lauryn Hill's *Doo Wop (That Thing)* and Aretha Franklin's *A Rose is Still a Rose*, which were being blasted from the sound system in the adjoining room. Most of the women were in their thirties and forties, Yassin reckoned, and this was their night, the one occasion, perhaps, where they could leave their circumscribed lives behind and surround themselves with like-minded people who wanted to dance, kiss, fuck and celebrate each other. Yassin was unexpectedly moved by all these women who had gathered in sisterhood and the general air of camaraderie between them.

To his surprise he noticed, in the far corner of the bar area, a group of young black men wearing pimp-type outfits: bowler hats, silver waistcoats, multi-coloured shirts, pin-striped trousers and crocodile-skin cowboy boots. There was nothing effeminate about these boyish men; if anything they looked as hard as hell. What were they doing in a lesbian bar? As soon as he asked himself this a group of pretty black women in tight skirts and towering stilettos, whom Savannah dismissed as 'lipstick femmes', sashayed by. The young men gave them flirtatious looks, to which the women responded with equally flirtatious smiles. Yassin was extremely puzzled. Why were these young men flirting with (what he presumed) were lesbians, and, just as interestingly, why were the lesbians flirting back? Was this some strange hallucination brought on by the weed he had consumed earlier? He turned to Savannah to ask her but she had already disappeared off to the dance-floor in the next room. In pursuit of her Yassin walked past the young pimp lookalikes. One of them gave a provocative flick of his tongue and said, 'Wha gwan sexy gyal,' but Yassin pretended he hadn't heard.

It was dark in the hall with only fluorescent lighting flickering erratically on the dancers' writhing bodies. As Yassin's eyes adjusted he could just about make out Savannah's gold lamé dress shimmering in the distance. She seemed immersed in her own world, her body driven by the slinky beat. The song was Alison Hinds' *Roll it Gal* and Yassin couldn't help but join Savannah. Together they danced like the music was a drug that fed their need for movement, freedom. Yassin closed his eyes drunkenly and swayed his body like a belly-dancer. As he grooved a stranger wrapped an arm around his waist, and before he knew it someone was grinding behind him. The overpowering scent of the person was Egoiste and Yassin would always associate that cologne with –

'Jude?' But when he turned around it was one of the pimp-looking young men he had seen by the bar. This particular guy had wide gap teeth and a small goatee. His T-shirt had a fluorescent Warner Brothers sign with the words, 'If You See Da Police, Warn a Brother' emblazoned on it. Yassin chuckled at the pun and playfully gyrated against the man's crotch. The man reached for Yassin's 'breasts' and felt him up. Yassin, driven by the beat, the weed and the alcohol, could only see Jude in his mind. As the young man caressed him Yassin imagined that it was Jude running his expert hands across his body. They danced like this for a while until the DJ stopped spinning the records.

'Ey, ladies,' she said over the crackling microphone, 'as you know here at Medusa we always try to give you your money's worth. We're not like them shady bars where you walk away at the end of the night feeling robbed. This sister I'm about to introduce is one of the baddest comedians out there, so without further ado, I want you to put your hands together and give it up for Ms. Gigi Tutuola!'

As the crowed clapped enthusiastically the young man with the gap teeth and the joke T-shirt grabbed Yassin's hand and led him back to the bar.

'What you drinkin', my halal soul sista?' asked the stranger in a young boy's tone. He sounded like a teenager whose voice hadn't yet cracked. Yassin sighed wistfully as he remembered Jude's baritone.

'JD and Coke,' he said, and as soon as he opened his

mouth, he realised his mistake.

'You're a fucking bloke?' said the young man, his face twisting in instant disgust.

'I don't know what *you're* chatting about,' scoffed Yassin. 'You're a straight guy fishing for chicks in a dyke bar. If that ain't lame, then I don't know what the fuck is.'

'You arsehole,' said the guy in his prepubescent voice before lifting his T-shirt to flash a firmly-bandaged chest that showed the faintest outline of flattened breasts. 'I *am* a fucking dyke!'

His face burning, Yassin stalked off to the smoking area. This was an alleyway behind the club with next to it a dog-pen that housed two pit-bulls, both of which began barking for his blood through the chicken wire. Holding back angry tears, Yassin tried to unbutton his blouse. When he couldn't succeed, he ripped the buttons off and threw the garment onto the ground. He then removed his hijab, crumpled it into a ball and flung it as far into the soulless night as he could. After a few moments of struggling with the bra clasp, he managed to tear the bra off too. Now he was wearing nothing but the uncomfortable jeans, and even those he unzipped all the way down until his genitals could breathe. Finally, he wiped furiously at his makeup until he resembled a mental patient with paint smudged across his face.

He stood in the cold, shivering, in that dark alley in Brixton, feeling crestfallen. What had he hoped to gain from this? He had tried going with the flow, going along with every strange situation that came his way. Every experience lately felt like an experiment of the body, of its power and limitations. Such experiments created a desire for something more fulfilling. It was a hunger born of rootlessness but he couldn't see that. He couldn't see that true liberation was a strictly DIY process, frightening in both its intensity and limitless scope. There seemed to be no boundaries between his male and female sides and this frightened him. Where to go next? How to embrace such complexity?

He would spend the rest of his life trying to answer that question. He stood in the cold being barked at by pit-bulls and watching cars go by and he knew he would make his way towards some higher ground, a place from which the view would be clearer, wider. His interior landscape was in transition. This night had been a dystopian fairytale but now the spell was broken and he had awoken. He licked his wounds and started walking home.

MY ROOTS ARE YOUR ROOTS

Korfa likes braiding marigolds in my dreadlocks because he says they remind him of home. He carries home in the way he walks: an elegant, loose strut. He wears home on his skin in the form of attar, a delicious perfume that makes me dream of Somali coastlines, places where children play football amidst colonial ruins, and young men like Korfa flee in darkness on boats to Yemen and Kenya, determined never to look back.

I am his only family in this country, and he braids marigold memories in my hair to share something of himself that is more intimate than an expensive bouquet of flowers. And at night he spreads his legs wide, arches his back and welcomes me into his tightness. I return the favour, expanding his erogenous zones with the tip of my tongue. I lick him until his abdominal muscles clench and his dick kicks and drips. He catches my every thrust until the bed collapses. I flex inside him on the floor and the warmth of his body is a gorgeous contrast to the cold wood floor hard against my kneecaps, my splaying, bracing toes. He groans and I grind deeper. He licks my lips. A bead of sweat from my forehead drops onto his nose and glints there, a diamante piercing. He runs his palms across my gleaming pectorals. Like an acrobat he wraps his legs around my waist, his arms around my shoulders, as, keeping inside him, I stand and lift him. As I turn him out, he grinds his buttocks up. And down. Up. And down. The rhythm has a thrill to it. I smell attar and sweat on his skin.

We always stroke until we're pure jazz and jizz. I whisper into the seashell of his ear, 'My roots are your roots.' We sleep to the sound of sirens speeding through the streets of Peckham.

I am Jamaican and Korfa is Somali. Neither of our families knows that we're two men who love each other. When we're together there is a sense of solace, a lack of fear. In the stickiness of city summer nights we open the windows wide, light incense. We make love and we forget. We forget that he comes from a country wrecked by war. He forgets that his family are still back home and in desperate need of money. He forgets the thrust and flow of daily life and we assume our own groove. I forget that my family would kill me if they found out. I forget that by loving Korfa my life is in danger. In those sticky summer nights in South London our windows stay open and our tiny apartment becomes our secret garden. The magic of the secret garden is that it exists in our imagination. There are no limits, no borderlines. The secret garden leads to the marigolds of Mogadishu and the magnolias of Kingston and when the heat turns us sticky and sweet and unwilling to be claimed by defeat we own the night. We own our bodies. We own our lives.

ACKNOWLEDGMENTS

I would like to offer my thanks to Monique Tomlinson, Kinsi Abdulleh, Osob Dahir, Lauren Trimble, Elmi Ali, Miriam Nice, Boris Mitkov and Sai Murray for their generosity of spirit and friendship. I would also like to extend my gratitude to my tutors at the Royal Holloway MA Creative Writing programme: Andrew Motion, Susanna Jones and Jo Shapcott. Special thanks to Mary Tierney, Dr Penny Ackland, Sokari Ekine, Matthew Todd, Colin Crummy, David Wolf, Billy Kahora, Angela Wachuka, Ellah Allfrey and Pam Nashel Leto for being champions. This book would not have been this book without your support. Thank you.

Lightning Source UK Ltd.
Milton Keynes UK
UKOW03f0231021014

239470UK00002B/9/P